Fourth and Ape
The Field Goal Kicker with the Secret Gorilla Leg

by Jeff Weiss

To Claire Lilienthal

Go Wolves !

Jeff Weiss

For Uncle John

The Gipper

"The Gipper" is the nickname given to George Gipp, a football player for Notre Dame (1918–1920). Gipp still holds several records for the Fighting Irish. The week before the big game against a formidable undefeated Army team, Gipp contracted strep throat and pneumonia. These were the days before antibiotics. From his deathbed, Gipp told coach Knute Rockne to tell the players to "win just one for the Gipper."

Rockne gave the famous "Win one for the Gipper" speech at halftime and the Fighting Irish rallied to beat Army 12–6. Since that time, the phrase "Win one for the Gipper" has been immortalized in football lore.

1.

Zeph and I stood in front of the elephant enclosure wondering where Ethel had gone. We were part of a ten-person team of Ellerbach High School students that had collected the most trash during City Cleanup day, winning first prize, a campout in the municipal zoo. We'd left football practice early to get an advanced viewing of the animals before the actual campout began.

"I see George," said Zeph, looking into the enclosure and shaking his head. "But I don't see Ethel."

"I hope she isn't loose," I said. "I don't want an elephant stomping on my tent in the middle of the night."

"Maybe I should wear my football equipment to bed," said Zeph.

Zeph and I had known each other since grade school. I was an animal lover and he was a football lover. It had been difficult to convince him to leave practice early. But now that we were in the zoo, he was glad we had the extra time to explore.

"There she is," said Zeph. "Behind that shed. She's standing up right now."

"Hi Ethel," I said. I talk to the animals, but they never seem to talk back to me. Indeed, the elephant did nothing to acknowledge my greeting. She just picked up a trunkful of hay, stuffed it in her mouth and chewed slowly.

"Mystery solved," said Zeph. "Let's see if the rest of the team is here."

"Let's go this way," I said. "It's just as quick and we'll get to see the otters."

The fall afternoon was warm and sunny, but as the sun descended in the sky, a small breeze picked up. We walked past the reptile house, which had a sign out front shaped like a giant snake.

"That reminds me," said Zeph. "Do you know what my brother told me?"

"What?"

"Check the toilet before you sit down. There might be an escaped rattlesnake hiding in there."

"Your brother is sinister!" I laughed.

"No kidding. He's trying to make me paranoid."

"A toilet is too wet for a rattlesnake. Anyway, I wouldn't worry about escaped animals. They're going to have this place on lockdown tonight. Especially with us teenagers staying here."

The river otters resided in a large enclosure with a bubbling stream running through the middle of it. We watched the otters play in the water for a few minutes, then walked around the corner and saw five tents pitched on a grassy area in the middle of the zoo.

"Wow, this is luxury," I said. They even pitched the tents for us."

"Sweet!" said Zeph.

I could barely wait for the evening tour. I'd been to the zoo countless times during the day, but never at night.

2.

Wild sounds pierced the air in the zoo that night. The jungle birds were cawing and the monkeys were howling. The leopards paced in their big enclosure, growling and roaring as the breeze gently shook the fronds of the palm trees. It was even spookier than I expected, but that was a good thing. I like spooky.

As the sun dipped under the horizon, we toured the zoo, making sure that we hit all the highlights: the rhinos, the polar bears, and the orangutans. We spent 15 minutes watching the penguins swim around in a large pool that was built like an underwater racetrack. We bet on which penguin would finish first. Everyone was declared a winner because we couldn't tell one penguin from another when it crossed the finish line.

Before we knew it, four hours had passed, and it was time to head back to the tents.

"C'mon, let's go," said the counselor. "Tomorrow you'll have about an hour to look around."

Everyone groaned. No one wanted to go back to the tents. It looked like there would be another half-hour of twilight, enough time to see the anteaters, the warthogs, and the meerkat colony. But the counselor was insistent. We were already a half-hour behind schedule, he said. We reluctantly walked toward the camping area.

The encampment was an odd but exciting sight in the middle of the zoo. The tents weren't big, and sharing mine with Zeph made it seem all the smaller. Zeph was 6 foot 3 inches tall and about 200 pounds, a great build for a high school linebacker. He'd worn his hair in a Mohawk earlier in the year, and now he was trying to grow out an Afro. It was taking forever and the remnants of the Mohawk were still showing.

I was several inches shorter than Zeph and weighed in at 178 pounds—and that was after beefing up for the football season. I was the second-string tight end and first-team punter and placekicker.

I kept my brown hair about six inches long and parted it on the left side or down the middle, depending on my mood. Sometimes I wore a sweatband under my helmet. Not because I sweated a lot. After all, I was the kicker, not the most strenuous of jobs. But the sweatband kept my hair in place when I put on my helmet.

Zeph and I were unrolling our sleeping bags and arranging things in the tent when I suddenly remembered the armadillos.

"Oh man," I said, pulling my toothbrush out of my backpack.

"What?" said Zeph, yanking up the leg of his pajamas.

"I forgot to take a picture of an armadillo."

"You can take the picture tomorrow. The counselor said we'd have an hour tomorrow to walk around the zoo."

"Armadillos sleep during the day. It'll probably be curled up in a ball tomorrow. Angie will think I took a picture of a dirt clod."

"That's what armadillos look like," said Zeph, "a big, round dirt clod."

"I'll just sneak out now and snap a quick picture. No one will know."

"I wouldn't do it if I were you," Zeph shook his head. "You'll be in major trouble if they find you wandering around the zoo after lights out."

"If anyone sees me, I'll just tell them that I'm heading to the bathroom."

"With your camera? Why don't you just use your cell phone camera? Do you really need a high-definition picture of an armadillo?"

"Yeah, I guess you're right," I said. I dropped the camera into my backpack and grabbed my cell phone.

Zeph looked at me suspiciously. "Something tells me that it's more than the armadillo. I think you want to go exploring."

I considered this for a moment. "Maybe," I said quietly.

"I'll do my best to cover for you, but I can't promise anything," he said.

"Do you want to come with me?"

"No."

"Alright. I shouldn't be gone too long," I said.

I hadn't expected Zeph to come along. He had enjoyed his night in the zoo, but he wasn't crazy about animals like I was. Zeph was motivated by sports, particularly football. He loved playing defense and was really looking forward to the game tomorrow with our cross-town rivals, the Jefferson Bearcats. Unfortunately, it hadn't been much of a rivalry lately, as we hadn't beat them in ten years.

But, Zeph and other members of the team were optimistic about this season. At 4-1, our current record was better than it had been in ten seasons. An impartial observer would say that the easy games had fallen early in the schedule, which may have been true. But hope springs eternal, and our team felt that maybe, just maybe, this would be the season that we'd put together a winning team. We'd see soon enough, the tough part of the season was coming up.

I liked football, but I wasn't crazy about it. Maybe it was because I didn't play all that much as the second-string tight end. As for the kicking game? Although our offense was getting better, we still punted a lot. If we scored a touchdown, I'd kick an extra point and the kickoff. But we hardly ever tried field goals. If I had been able to attempt a few more field goals, the games would have been a lot more exciting for me. But Coach didn't seem to think that field goals should be an important part of the high school game, so I mostly practiced punting and extra points.

I guess if I were more like Zeph – excited about football - I would have stayed in the tent. But as a punter and extra point kicker, I didn't see much action.

I was, however, very interested in animals. So, it was time to let the armadillo adventure begin.

3.

I stuck my head out of the tent to see if any of the counselors
were lurking outside. The coast was clear.

"If you see a bearcat, kick it for me," said Zeph.

"A bearcat?" I said, turning around to look at him.

"I'm kidding. We're playing the Bearcats tomorrow,
remember?"

"Oh, right," I chuckled.

"You better hurry," he said.

"Right. I'm going now," I said. "But first I'm going to stop
by the bathroom. I need to use it before I start on my little
adventure."

"You owe me one," said Zeph shaking his finger. I could see
a faint I-can't-believe-you're-doing-this smile across his face.
Very faint.

I hopped out of the tent and jogged to the restrooms. In the
stall, I couldn't help it: I checked for rattlesnakes in the toilet. Of
course, there were none to be found. I took out my cell phone and

snapped a picture of the toilet so Zeph could show his brother later.

I peeked outside the men's room, looking both ways, then scurried past the tent encampment. I headed toward the armadillo enclosure, which turned out to be a lot farther from the tents than I remembered. I walked briskly and stuck to the side of the walkways, trying to stay in the shadows. A few sidewalk lights cast an amber glow and a half moon shone in the night sky.

Finally, I arrived at the armadillo cage. The bony-plated animal was curled in a ball, fast asleep.

"Aren't you supposed to be nocturnal?" I said.
The creature was in no mood for conversation and reacted by sticking its nose out for a second, sniffing a few times, and slowly curling into a tighter ball. I looked further into the cage and saw a second armadillo near a small pile of brush. It was rolled in a ball, too.

I snapped a couple of pictures, then wandered to the buffalo enclosure. I don't know why it surprised me, but the buffaloes had enormous heads and huge nostrils. All the same, they were noble-looking beasts and I took a couple of pictures.

I meandered past the reptile house to the gorilla exhibit.

I'd been to the zoo a couple of weeks earlier and had been disappointed by the absence of the big silverback gorilla. That's not to say that the other gorillas weren't impressive, but the silverback was enormous and fierce-looking, a real showstopper.

As I stood in front of the gorilla enclosure, I saw that the silverback was still gone. I looked around for some note of explanation, but I found nothing. And I hadn't read anything about it on the zoo blog, which I read every week.

I peered into the enclosure at the remaining gorillas. Three gorillas, a female and two juveniles, were standing on all fours on a dirt patch in the middle of the exhibit. The big, muscular primates had noticed me and stood motionless, staring at me. We looked at each other for a long time. I wondered what they were thinking. It's funny, when a gorilla stares at you, it's not as uncomfortable as when a human stares at you. Maybe it doesn't occur to them that it's rude to stare. So, you don't feel like you have to be polite either.

Or maybe they weren't being rude—maybe they were trying to communicate with me, I suddenly thought.

I tried a little telepathy, trying to send my thoughts to the gorillas. "Hello, gorillas. What would you like to tell me?"

The gorillas just kept staring back at me.

I concentrated again. "How do you like your enclosure?"

No response again.

"Is the food okay? If you had a choice of anything to eat, what would it be?"

Despite my best efforts, I couldn't get a telepathic response from the gorillas. Oh, well, I decided. It had been worth the try.

The gorillas continued to stare at me. I wondered if they were upset about the absence of the silverback.

I concentrated again, trying to send my thoughts to the gorillas. "Are you worried about your companion?"

The gorillas stared, while I kept trying to pick up the vibe. I could have stayed there another hour or so, but I had limited time and lots of the zoo to see. As I walked away, I waved to the gorillas, but again, they just stared.

As I rounded the zebra enclosure, I saw a large three-story brick building that seemed to jut straight up from the surrounding grounds. This was a zoo, after all, and a three-story brick building seemed like it belonged downtown, not in the midst of all the animal enclosures. The building was dark except for one window on the second floor. From the window, a blue light spilled onto the sidewalk.

As I neared the building, I noticed a green metal sign riveted to the wall with the words "Veterinary Hospital" written on it. Well, that made sense. I looked up at the blue light pouring out of the window. It wasn't unusual that someone would be working late; the animal hospital was a very busy place. But I was a little disturbed by a strange noise coming from the building. It sounded like snoring—deep, heavy snoring. Then suddenly the snoring stopped, and it was quiet once again.

Hmmm, I thought. *Maybe I should check it out.* As I tiptoed up the stone stairs toward the front door, it occurred to me that this was one of the dumber ideas that I'd had. What business did I have going into the veterinary hospital when I was supposed to be in my tent? I was just asking for trouble. I laughed at myself and turned around and headed in the direction of the campsite.

The walk back to the tents was a long one, and I should have hurried along, but I meandered. After all, when would a chance like this come along again? I should take advantage of this opportunity, I mused to myself as I strolled along under the moonlight.

When I neared the petting zoo, the goats and sheep trotted over to the fence. It didn't take me long to realize they wanted food. *Oh, why not?* I thought. I stuck a quarter in the food dispenser and turned the crank. Suddenly, out of the corner of my eye, I noticed a small shape moving on the sidewalk in the distance. It was headed my direction. I couldn't tell what it was, but whatever it was, it was moving fast.

A chill ran up my spine. I didn't know what animal it might be, but it was running toward me, perhaps a sign that it was aggressive or just plain crazy. Maybe it was a wild, desperate animal that had tunneled under its fence. My mind raced. I cast my eyes around, looking for a tree to climb or something to grab to ward off the fast-approaching mystery beast.

I thought about jumping over the fence into the petting zoo, but I figured the small fence wouldn't stop the marauding beast. Finally, I decided that I would jump on top of the trash receptacle, and kick at the animal if it attacked me. But the animal was moving too fast. Before I even took two steps, it had arrived. It was a medium-size monkey, maybe a howler or a macaque. The monkey jumped on me and quickly scrambled up my body, as if I were a small tree.

"Yeow! Get off me!" I shouted.

The monkey grabbed my cap and leapt over my head. I turned around to see the furry demon sprinting down the walkway with my cap in its hands.

My heart was still pounding a mile a minute, but beneath the fright was a feeling of relief. I hadn't been involved in a life and death struggle with a wild animal. I hadn't been bloodied by sharp claws. Nor had I received a savage bite from a frothy-mouthed rabid beast. I let out a couple of long breaths and wiped the sweat from my forehead.

My next emotion was a peculiar sense of outrage. To tell the truth, I almost laughed. It was such a bizarre occurrence. But at the same time I was mad that the monkey had stolen my favorite cap.

"Get back here, monkey. Give me my cap!" I shouted. I quickly realized the futility of yelling at the monkey. Also, I was making an unholy racket in the middle of the zoo when I was supposed to be in my tent. I looked around to see if I had drawn the attention of anyone. Not a soul in sight.

So I took off after the little thief.

The monkey was incredibly fast. Had the cap been an ordinary one, I would have given up the chase and returned to my tent with a great tale about a baseball cap–stealing monkey. The stolen cap would have been a small price to pay for such an outstanding story. But this was my Red Devils cap. The Red Devils had been the original name for my high school team before it split into two schools. The new team names were the Bulldogs and the Coyotes. There were no more Red Devils, and no more Red Devils caps. My cap was a piece of history. Everyone at the school wanted to buy it from me, but I never sold it. I treasured that cap.

So I sprinted down the sidewalk after the monkey. He was way ahead of me and I wasn't sure I could catch him.

Then the monkey did an incredible thing. He whipped around to face me, let out a loud shriek, and jumped up and down, taunting me like a nasty little demon. Then he turned and ran down the long walkway toward the veterinary hospital. He bounded up a tall juniper tree, swung through an open second-story window, and vanished.

"Oh, great," I said. "There goes my favorite cap."

4.

As I neared the building, I could see the blue light still glowing on the second floor. I checked the door. It was locked. I grabbed a soda straw that was lying on the ground, folded it in half, and stuck it between the double doors, trying to move the locking mechanism. Ridiculous. The straw wasn't nearly sturdy enough.

I crept around the other side of the building. *Aha!* There was an open window. *Didn't anyone close windows in this place?* As luck would have it, this open window was also next to a tree—a medium-sized oak, not a flimsy juniper. So I seized the opportunity. I pulled myself up by the lowest branch and climbed onto the limb that extended toward the window. As I scooted along the limb, I could hear it creaking and moaning under my weight. The window wasn't open wide enough to climb through, so I slowly began lifting it, trying to be as quiet as possible and careful not to shift my weight too rapidly for fear that the branch might break and send me crashing to the ground.

A sudden loud, horrendous sound broke out underneath me.

"Squaaaawk!"

I lurched upwards, smacking my head on the branch above me. *Wow, did that ever hurt!* I blinked my eyes a few times and watched tiny stars slowly pass back and forth before my eyes. I looked toward the ground. Finally focusing my eyes, I saw a peacock.

"Squaaaawk!"

Oh, he was a noisy, arrogant fellow, proudly fanning his tail feathers.

"Get out of here," I hissed at him. "Can't you see I'm trying to break into a building?"

"Squaaaawk!"

"Quiet," I said. But the peacock made no sign that he had heard me or cared that I was struggling to break into the building *Could there be a worse time for a peacock encounter?* The noise was certain to draw attention to me. I was a sitting duck. I waited for a few moments, frozen in fear, waiting for someone to see me and call the zoo authorities, who would certainly cart me off to jail. Heck, they wouldn't even have to throw me in jail; they could just toss me in one of the animal cages.

But no one came to the window. No one walked down the sidewalk either. Then I realized that a squawking peacock in the zoo was no more unusual than a cawing blue jay in someone's backyard or a mooing cow on a farm. I smiled a smug smile, feeling quite superior to the peacock.

I quickly went back into action, trying to open the window. With some effort, I yanked it up, making an opening that seemed wide enough for me to squeeze through. I pushed off from the branch and tried to scoot headfirst through the window like a snake slithering through a space in a woodpile. I could hear the tree branch creaking and I tried to shift most of my weight onto the windowsill, but I was stuck between the branch and the window. Even the peacock sensed the danger and strutted away from the branch.

Turned out that the peacock wasn't so dumb, for suddenly the tree limb cracked like a thunderclap and crashed to the ground with a great thud.

5.

The sound of the cracking limb frightened me so much that I lunged forward with all my might and tumbled through the window onto the floor, knocking a soda bottle from the top of a desk. Luckily, the bottle was plastic and empty. But it bounced, *doink-doink-doink*ing across the floor. I couldn't have possibly made more noise.

I leapt to my feet and looked around the office, listening for footsteps that I was certain would be coming down the hall. I heard none. I peered out the window of the office door, and saw no one. I let out a long breath, grateful that I hadn't been discovered.

I was safe. So far. Now I had to find the monkey! I paused for a moment to consider my course of action.

Then the cold hard facts hit me like a ton of bricks. Here I was out after curfew, breaking into a building to get my baseball cap back from a thieving monkey. And what if I did find the monkey? He could be with people, who would demand to know how I'd gotten into the building. They'd certainly call the police and I'd end up in jail. Or maybe they would take matters into their own hands. Maybe they'd just throw me to the bears.

Sweat beaded up on my forehead. I wondered if the counselors would do a bed check and realize that I was missing. My worries were piling up. Suddenly losing my Red Devils cap seemed like the least of my troubles. If I were caught in a locked zoo hospital after lights out my high school football career would be *finito!* It would mean a yearlong detention. My parents would send me to a reform school.

I had to get out of the building as soon as possible. But how? The tree branch was gone and it was too high to jump. No, the window wouldn't work. I'd have to go through the front door. I'd just have to be careful not to be seen sneaking through the building.

I mustered my nerve and peered into the hallway to consider my escape route. I saw blue light spilling out of the windows of a set of double doors. "Oh great," I whispered to myself. To get to the front stairway, I would have to walk past the room with the eerie blue light.

The room was about halfway down the hall. To keep from being seen, I would need to crawl beneath the windows of the double doors. I'd have to be careful, but I could do it. That was my plan.

As I tiptoed into the hallway, I was stopped in my tracks by a couple of loud snores, the same loud snoring that I had heard earlier. Next, a couple of loud snorts pierced the air and just as suddenly the snoring stopped. I heard a man's voice coming from the room with the blue light. I stood up straight with fright.

"Where did you get that hat, Ipoo?" said the voice.

"Bleeek!" shrieked the monkey. I cringed. The nasty little devil was the source of all my troubles. Okay, maybe I shouldn't have snuck out of my tent, and maybe I shouldn't have broken into the building. But I was just a trespasser. He was a thief.

I wondered what kind of people were in the room. I was getting a very bad feeling. I continued to tiptoe down the hall, scooting between potted plants and staying in the shadows. I neared the doors and noticed that they were the swinging kind, the type that are used in surgical units. My curiosity got the best of me: I tried to peer through the porthole windows into the room. From the right angle in the dark hallway, I figured I could see into the room without the occupants seeing me. I just had to know what was going on in the room with the blue light.

6.

I was astonished at what I saw. Lying on an operating table in the center of the room was the giant silverback gorilla—his massive body sprawled out, his large head tilted to the side, and his eyes looking like they were staring right at me.

But the gorilla wasn't seeing anything. He was fast asleep. He smacked his lips and made a chewing motion and began to snore. *Fascinating,* I thought. *So that's where the loud snoring was coming from.* And that's why the giant silverback wasn't in his enclosure. A very interesting story, one that I could tell my friends later, but first I had to get out of there.

As I bent down, preparing to crawl along the floor, a long, dark shadow loomed over me.

"Looking for something?" said a deep voice in what sounded like a German accent.

I jumped up and turned around to behold a huge man dressed in a white lab coat looking me straight in the eye. He must have been six-foot-seven and 275 pounds. He was square-jawed and not unattractive, but in my state of mind, it felt like I was having a firsthand encounter with Frankenstein. And Frankenstein's eyes were lit up and he was grinning at me menacingly.

"I, ah, well…" I started. My mind was working at warp speed. *Why the heck hadn't I thought of an excuse in case I got caught?* "Er, aaa, well, you see," I stammered. The giant continued to stare at me, his grin widening with my increasing agitation. "Well, I know it sounds strange, but a monkey stole my cap," I finally blurted out.

"That does sound a little strange," said the behemoth. "But not as strange as a boy in the zoo hospital after dark." He grinned again, shaking his massive head back and forth.

I got a sinking feeling that it was going to be a long night.

7.

"I didn't sneak into the zoo," I pleaded, looking at the giant man standing before me. "Really. I'm here as part of a school trip. You see, we had an auction, a silent auction, and—"

Before I could finish, he grabbed me under the arms, lifted me up, and slammed me through the swinging double doors like a fullback crashing through a defensive line.

A blond-haired man of medium build with brown horn-rimmed glasses was in the lab, holding up a syringe. Our abrupt entrance surprised him, and he looked at me quizzically over the top of his glasses.

It was then that I locked eyes with the thieving monkey, who began prancing around the room with my cap in its hands.

"Woooo!" shouted the monkey.

"Who is this?" said the blond-haired man, pointing a syringe at me.

"Some nosy kid," said the big guy with the German accent. He dropped his hands from under my armpits, and my feet hit the floor with a small thud. The big guy took a step forward and brushed his fingernails against his shirt as if he were proud of capturing me. "I caught him in the hallway. He was peeking through the laboratory windows."

"I was...ah...I was looking for my cap," I stammered.

"Ah, so it's *your* cap that Ipoo has stolen. I was wondering where he got it," said the blond-haired man, nodding his head. "Naughty monkey." The man shook his finger at Ipoo. "Would you give the hat back to the boy, Ipoo?"

The monkey hooted, jumped around in a circle, and sat on the cap. He shook his head from side to side. *"Bleeeck,* he shrieked.

The blond-haired man let out a deep breath. "I'm sorry. Ipoo is a bit uncooperative today. My name is Doctor Carlson. And this is Elko," he said, pointing at the big guy. "What is your name?"

"It's Ivan," I said.

"Just Ivan?"

"No, it's Ivan Zelinka."

"Is that Russian?" said Elko. "Are you a spy?" "Who sent you over here?"

"No, it's a Czech last name," I said.

"Czech, you say?" said Elko, looking me over, rubbing his chin. "Doesn't sound Czech to me."

"Sorry about your hat, Ivan," said Dr. Carlson, ignoring Elko.

"It's okay," I said. "You can mail it to me. I really need to get back to the tents."

"Tents?" said Dr. Carlson.

"Yes, I'm with a group of high school kids who are staying overnight in the zoo. So, if you'll excuse me…"

"Not so fast, kid," said the Elko, blocking the doorway. "Boss, do you think I should teach this kid a lesson?"

"No, no, Elko. If something were to happen to him there would be police swarming this place." Dr. Carlson chuckled. "We don't need that."

Dr. Carlson looked at the syringe in his hand and then peered over his glasses. "After all, we aren't doing anything wrong. We're just removing an appendix from this gorilla." Dr. Carlson winked at Elko.

Dr. Carlson rapped the syringe with his fingernail and held it in the air. He looked like he was anxious to get back to work. "Elko, would you get the boy's hat from Ipoo and escort him out?"

The monkey didn't like it when I got near him, but he really got upset when Elko approached him. Ipoo literally went ape, jumping up and down and shrieking. Then he lurched forward, escaping Elko's grasp, and plowed into Dr. Carlson's outstretched arm—the arm holding the syringe.

"Get off of me, you cursed monkey," shouted Dr. Carlson, swinging his arm. The syringe flew out of his hand, sailed across the room like a dart, and landed point down in my right leg.

"Yeow!" I shouted, staring at the syringe as it swayed back and forth on the needle that was stuck in my leg. The needle jab didn't hurt as much as it surprised me. It felt a little bit like a bee sting. I reached down and yanked the syringe out of my leg. I grabbed it from the top and I felt the palm of my hand slightly—almost imperceptibly—push down upon the plunger.

Dr. Carlson gave me a wide-eyed stare, a look of shock that sent a chill deep into my bones. Before I could say anything, he ran over to me, grabbed the syringe, and held it up to the light, closely examining the contents.

"Hmmm. It doesn't look like any serum is missing," he said in a strange, hurried tone that made me instantly doubt him. "I don't think you have anything to worry about."

He wasn't convincing me at all. Now I was really beginning to worry. "What is in that syringe?" I blurted.

Dr. Carlson stared at me for a moment. It appeared as if he were about to say something but thought better of it. The room was quiet, even Ipoo was staring at me without making a sound. I heard the clock ticking on the wall.

Finally, Elko broke the silence. "It's none of your business, kid."

"Quiet, Elko!" snapped Dr. Carlson. "I need to think."

Dr. Carlson sat down, slowly rubbed his forehead, and spoke. "Son, there is nothing wrong with the appendix of the gorilla lying on the table. We are performing research on a tropical disease. It's caused by a virus that is deadly to humans, but gorillas seem to be immune to it."

"Don't tell me you've injected me with a deadly virus!"

"No, no, no. I assure you it's nothing like that," said Dr. Carlson, wiping his brow. "Let me continue. We are involved in some top secret research. A few of our special agents were exposed to the virus while on a mission in a location that will remain nameless—for security purposes."

"What were they doing?" I asked.

"None of your business, kid," said Elko again.

Dr. Carlson waved him off and continued. "I can only tell you that they were overseas and were exposed to the virus while working there. We don't know if they acquired the disease or not, but we are working on a cure just in case."

"So you injected me with the cure?"

"No, it's not the cure. We are still working on the cure. We're in the research stage right now." He paused and looked at the syringe again. "It's nothing to worry about. I really don't think any of the serum got into your leg."

"But what is it?"

"We drew some genetic material from the gorilla and mixed it with growth hormone. We were going to make a batch of gorilla cells for research."

"Gorilla cells?"

"Yes, gorilla cells and 1,700 percent growth hormone."

"Seventeen-hundred percent growth hormone?" I didn't like the sound of that.

"We need lots of cells, so we are using the growth hormone to cause the gorilla cells to replicate at 1,700 times their normal rate. I've developed my own, shall we say, booster. The booster makes the whole thing biologically possible."

"Are you sure none of that solution got into me?"

"It didn't. I'm looking at it right now." Dr. Carlson held up the syringe again to the light. "It doesn't look like any is missing. I know exactly how much I had in here."

"And what would happen if some did get into me?"

"You'd turn into a gorilla, kid," said Elko. "Better get used to walking on your knuckles." He burst into laughter.

"What!?"

"Don't listen to him," said Dr. Carlson. "There's little chance of you turning into a gorilla. The experiments that we did on mice were all failures."

"Failures?" That didn't sound comforting to me either.

"I mean to say, the mice didn't develop gorilla attributes." Dr. Carlson paused for a moment to consider. "Of course, humans are much more closely related to gorillas. And as I've said, there are some boosters in the serum that make it more effective on humans. After this top secret business is finished, I may get a patent on it."

Dr. Carlson beamed proudly. I didn't know what to say. I just stared at him.

"What happened to the mice? Did they live?" I demanded, although I wasn't sure I wanted to hear the answer.

"They gave their last full measure for science," spouted Elko. Then he laughed.

"What's that supposed to mean?" I could literally feel my eyes bug-out as a cold wave of dread shot through my body.

"Oh, don't worry," said Dr. Carlson, waving his hands. "You're positively enormous compared to a mouse. And physically much more closely related to a gorilla. If by some remote chance some of the serum got into your muscle tissue, you might notice some small changes. You could feel a little restless or you might feel a little giddy or hungry. Who knows? But if you notice anything significant, call me at once."

Dr. Carlson handed me his card. He turned around, wiped the end of the syringe with an alcohol pad, and set it down on the counter. Then he turned back to me. "As I said, this is top secret. No one is to know. Not even your parents. We are doing very important government research. You don't want to spend Halloween in jail, do you? Of course not," he said. "Now go back to your tent and go to sleep, and forget any of this happened."

After jabbing me with a syringe full of who-knows-what, they were trying to get rid of me.

"Wait a minute. What's top secret about this? As the patient, I demand to know," I said, surprising myself. I think I had watched too many doctor dramas on TV.

My little spark of attitude wasn't lost on Elko. "Should I crush him into a ball, Doc?" he asked.

Dr. Carlson slowly looked me over, as if crushing me into a ball were a scientific experiment he was considering. "No, no, Elko, I'll tell him. Once he knows the importance of what we are doing, it will help him keep his mouth shut."

I sat down on a creaky lab chair and waited for my explanation. In the meantime, Ipoo cackled and rubbed the top of his head. He tried to put on my cap, but since it was too large, he laid it on the table and sat on it. *What kind of researchers would allow a crazy monkey in their laboratory?* I wondered.

"The men and women who were exposed to this disease were special agents on a top secret mission," said Dr. Carlson. "They have been quarantined, because we are unsure of severity of this disease. We don't know how contagious it is, and therefore we cannot risk exposing the general population. We are not sure if any of the agents have contracted the disease. But as a precaution, Elko and I are working on a cure. And the cure lies within that gorilla lying on the table.

"No one knows about the mission except for a few people, including you. Exposing the disease would mean revealing the mission and creating an international incident."

My mind was spinning. "You mean to tell me that you are working on a top secret mission in this crummy little lab?"

"Boss, I still like the idea of crushing him into a ball," said Elko.

"It may not look like it to you, but we are in the midst of some groundbreaking research here," said Dr. Carlson.

"Well, how do you know that gorillas are immune?" I asked.

"I've been doing research on primates for years. Besides the obvious attributes, they have many similarities to human beings."

Dr. Carlson made a steeple with his fingers and nodded his head. "Indeed, I've learned the quirks and personalities of hundreds of primates. For example, that gorilla lying in front of us seems calm enough, doesn't he?"

I nodded my head, unsure why he was asking.

"Well, I can tell you right now that he is having a very troubling dream," said Dr. Carlson. "I can tell by looking at him, even from over here."

Well, if the gorilla was having a troubling dream, I sure couldn't tell. In fact, I was a bit envious of the great ape. He looked quite serene to me. And even if he were having a bad dream, when he woke up his troubles would be over.

Unlike me, whose troubles were just beginning.

8.

"Ba-rooaar!"

The giant silverback sat up on the operating table, his eyes ablaze, his muscles flexed and bulging. His teeth were big, shiny and white. He had broken one of this arm restraints and he was swinging and clutching at the air, assailing anything that would be foolish or unfortunate enough to get within his grasp.

I nearly jumped out of my shoes. I took two steps toward the door, but Elko grabbed me by my shirt collar and yanked me back. I couldn't break his grip. I whipped my neck around to see the gorilla settling back on the table and returning to his slumber. Elko released his hold on my shirt and stood looking at the gorilla, nodding his head as if in approval.

"He does that all the time," said Elko. "I think he has a bad dream from time to time. Nothing to worry about. He's gone back to sleep."

Easy for him to say. I had no experience standing next to a roaring gorilla and I would have been down the hall and halfway across the zoo if Elko hadn't grabbed me.

Dr. Carlson walked over to the silverback and leaned over the gorilla's head, probably to assess his breathing. "It might have been a bad dream, but it won't be long before he wakes up. We'd better hurry," said Dr. Carlson. "And I think we might need to fix the arm restraint."

I was having a difficult time calming down after the gorilla outburst. The arm he'd been waving around seemed as big as an oak tree. When he'd roared, he'd opened his mouth so wide I'm sure someone could have stuffed a cantaloupe inside. But who would have wanted to do that? His canine teeth were as long as my index finger and probably sharp as nails. Finally, I collected myself long enough to speak.

"So, I've been injected with this gorilla's genes?" I pointed at the gorilla on the table.

"Why kid, is there *another* gorilla you're particularly fond of?" said Elko. He let out a sly laugh.

"Yes," said Dr. Carlson. "He's generally a rather pleasant fellow, except for when he has a bad dream."

"Or when he goes on a rampage," said Elko, chuckling.

"Rampage?"

"Elko, stop it," snapped Dr. Carlson. "I've said enough, perhaps too much, and I've really got to get back to this gorilla.

Call me if you notice any changes. And just for good measure, here's an annual membership to the zoo," he said, handing me a card that he pulled from his lab coat. "Elko, see him out."

"Let's go, kid," said Elko, walking toward me.

"What about my cap? I have to get my hat back from that monkey."

"His name is Ipoo," said Elko, pronouncing the syllables EYE-POO very distinctly. "He's named after the city in Malaysia where he was born."

"The city is Ipoh and it's actually pronounced EE-POE, but never mind," said Dr. Carlson. We've been calling him EYE-POO for so long, there's no need to change it now.

Elko nodded his head at this statement and gave a little snort through his nose, as if he wanted to say something snarky. Once again, I wondered about the competency of these scientists who allowed a monkey in their laboratory, a monkey whose named they had screwed up.

Elko walked over to a refrigerator and pulled an ice cream sandwich out of the freezer compartment. "Here ya go, Ipoo." Elko waved the ice cream sandwich in the air. The monkey approached slowly, apprehensively. Elko quickly grabbed an aerosol can from the top of the table. *Psssssssst!* He sprayed Ipoo squarely in the face. The monkey shrieked and ran over to the corner, keeling over like a bundle of sticks being dropped on the floor.

Elko walked over and grabbed my cap, then handed it to me. "Here's your hat," he said.

I must have looked shocked. I *was* shocked, so shocked that Elko walked over and put his hand on my shoulder.

"Don't worry, kid. He'll sleep it off in a couple of hours. Then he can have the ice cream sandwich," said Elko, leading me out the door.

9.

"Where the heck have you been?" said Zeph as I slipped into the tent. "I was about to get the counselor to look for you. I thought you fell into the bear cage."

I looked at Zeph remorsefully. "Did anyone notice that I was gone?" I asked.

"No, you're lucky. I was about to get a search party together." Zeph looked me over for a second or two. "You look terrible. What happened to you?"

My mind raced for something to say without revealing the so-called secret mission. "A monkey stole my Red Devils cap."

"A monkey stole your cap?" said Zeph in disbelief. "A monkey running loose in the zoo?"

"Maybe a macaque or a howler."

"Uh-huh," said Zeph. "A howler monkey stole your cap."

"Or a macaque."

"That's interesting because while you were away, a giraffe stole my pants," said Zeph. "He gave them back to me because they didn't fit."

Obviously, Zeph didn't believe my story. Could I blame him? "I know it sounds farfetched. This wasn't a zoo monkey. It was someone's pet monkey. His name is Ipoo."

"Ipoo?" said Zeph, shaking his head. "Ipoo, the monkey,"

"Ipoh is a city in Malaysia. Well, it's actually pronounced a little differently. But that's where the monkey was born. So he's probably a macaque. It's a long story. I'll try to explain it to you someday. Right now we should keep our voices down and get to bed. I'm sorry I made you worry."

Zeph shook his head. It seemed like he was tired and wanted to get to bed. "Well, as far as I can tell, you got away with it. No one except me knew you were gone. You're lucky."

"I guess I am," I said.

But the truth was, I didn't feel very lucky at all. I had just been jabbed in the leg with a syringe containing gorilla genes, 1,700 percent growth hormone and some top secret booster serum. And the worst part about it was these nutty scientists wanted me to keep it a secret. I wondered how long I could pull that off.

10.

The next morning I awoke wondering if it had all been a dream. Most of the campers had arisen before me, and I could hear them rummaging around outside. Through the tent opening, I could see Zeph milling about near some portable stoves.

Suddenly I bolted straight up in my sleeping bag. *My leg! What about my leg. It's been stabbed with a syringe full of gorilla serum!* I sprang out of my sleeping bag, pulled down my pajamas, and examined my leg from foot to thigh. I ran my hands up and down my calf and thigh, feeling for any strange bumps or lumps. Finally, I let out a sigh of relief. It looked more or less normal. I couldn't even tell where the syringe had stuck me. I lay back down on my sleeping bag and stared at the tent ceiling. What a relief!

I put on my clothes and wandered outside. Zeph was talking to one of the zookeepers. He saw me, but he continued his conversation. I chatted with a couple of the other students as I ate a couple bowls of instant oatmeal. It wasn't long before the bus arrived to take us home. Just as I suspected, we weren't going to get the extra hour that morning to explore the zoo.

I'd had enough of exploring anyway.

At home, I gave my family a heavily edited story about my night in the zoo. I told them some of my experiences: the calls of the toucans, the lazy armadillos, and the racing penguins. Of course, I mentioned nothing of the building with the blue light, the monkey named Ipoo, or the gorilla serum with 1,700 percent growth hormone.

"That sounds wonderful," Mom said.

"Wonderful, yes," I said.

You should write it up for the school newspaper," she said.

"Maybe I should," I said. I wanted to tell the full, unedited version. That would be a load off my mind. But I couldn't tell that story without revealing the secret mission.

"Hey, it's time to get ready for the football game," said Dad.

"Okay, I'll get changed," I said and went into my bedroom.

It might seem strange that I would get dressed at home to play in a football game. However, if you had ever seen our locker room at the stadium, you would know why. It was a beat-up, dingy space with rusty-hinged locker doors, grimy showers, and bare bulbs hanging from electric cords.

Of course, football players are supposed to be tough and not afraid of getting dirty, but everyone was grossed out by the peeling paint, dirty walls, and mouse droppings underneath the lockers. As a result, most players dressed at home and brought a change of clothing for after the game. The showers were rarely used, because once you stepped out of the shower onto the grungy floor, you felt like you had to get back into the shower to get clean again. So, I got ready at home.

I suited up in full pads, jersey, and pants and walked outside to the end of the driveway. I climbed in the rattletrap that passed for my car and headed toward Logan Field for the game.

11.

Our team, the Bulldogs, jogged onto the field, did some stretching exercises, and ran a couple of pass patterns. I did a couple of stretches and practiced kicking the ball into a net. We huddled together on the sidelines, arms around one another's shoulder pads.

"One, two, three! Beat the Bearcats!" we shouted and dashed onto the field to a smattering of applause from the stands, which were half full. Not bad for a team that hadn't beaten its cross-town rival for the past ten years.

We lost the coin toss, so we would kick off to the Bearcats. That meant that I, as the team placekicker, would be a central part of the first play. Sometimes I got nervous when I was the first to kick off. But once I got onto the field with my teammates, my nervousness usually changed into eagerness.

I trotted onto the field and placed the ball on the tee at the 40-yard line. I inhaled deeply, taking in the familiar scent of the sod on the field. I jogged back to the 30-yard line where my teammates were lined up. I raised my hand in the air, signaling that I was ready to kick. Then I ran full speed at the ball and kicked it hard.

I don't know if my ankle was stiff or if I was too anxious, but instead of kicking the ball in the lower third, where I was supposed to, I kicked it in the middle. It zinged forward end over end, took a freaky bounce, and landed near the 30-yard line, where is continued to bounce so erratically that the Bearcats had a hard time fielding it. Eventually, one of their players grabbed it and ran the ball back to the 35-yard line before being tackled.

I jogged over to the bench and started to stretch my leg and ankle.

"A strange but lucky bounce," said Tommy Dittmore, the halfback, sitting on the bench with the other offensive players. He was not really my favorite person on the team, a glory hound, always wanting the ball and complaining when he didn't get it.

"My leg is stiff," I said. "I'm working it out right now. Next one will be off the ground." I turned around to watch the game.

Unfortunately, the Bearcats were making good yardage on most plays. We got a few good defensive stops, but then they called a draw play that fooled everyone. Their halfback ran it in for a touchdown. Perhaps as annoying as the touchdown were the cheers coming from the stands. It seemed like there were as many

Bearcat fans as Bulldog fans, and this was our home field.

The Bearcats kicked off. Tommy stood at the 15-yard line, waiting for the ball. He got a few good blocks, dodged a player or two, and ran it out to the 30-yard line. The rest of the offense jogged onto the field. But, they couldn't produce. After three lackluster plays, Coach called me out to punt the ball.

I lined up ten yards behind Reggie Mapu, our center. Reggie was a big Samoan guy, with the strength, quickness and agility that made him a great center. He was an excellent blocker, fast off the ball. Most of all, he had great hands and always snapped the ball right at the numbers on my jersey.

"Ninety-nine, 45, hut, hut, hut, HUT!" I called and stomped my foot.

Reggie didn't disappoint this time either. The ball landed right in my hands.

One step, two steps, BOOM! I punted the ball. My leg shot straight upward, and my foot hit the ball with a wallop. I watched with bewilderment as the ball shot straight up into the air, gaining altitude until it looked like a small speck against the sky. Eventually, it came sailing back to earth, gathering speed, getting bigger and bigger as it approached the field.

WHAP! The ball landed five yards downfield from the line of scrimmage. There was laughter from the stands: with all that distance upward, the ball had traveled only 15 yards from the place where I punted it. Luckily, it bounced along for 12 yards before one of our players downed it at the 45-yard line.

I jogged off the field, meeting our defensive players as they ran onto the field.

"What the heck?" said Jonesy, the outside linebacker. "That was the highest punt I've ever seen." He paused for a moment. "It was also the shortest punt I've ever seen."

"Wow, you creamed that baby," said Middlebury, the safety, laughing as he ran onto the field. "I've never seen anything like that. Try pointing your toe next time."

He was right. One of my ankle joints seemed very stiff. I walked to an empty spot on the sidelines and knelt on the turf, with the tops of my feet flat on the grass behind me. This hurt a little bit, but soon I could feel the stretch working. I pushed down for about 30 or 40 seconds then stood back up, feeling good and loose. But when I pulled down my socks to massage my right calf, I was shocked to see tufts of long black hair growing out of my skin. I stared at it in horror and disbelief. Then I quickly pulled up my sock, looking around to make sure no one had just seen what I had seen.

Thoughts rushed through my head like a high-speed train. Cold sweat beaded up on my forehead. *Was I growing a gorilla leg?* The idea seemed preposterous and strange, like something you'd read about in a comic book.

I sat down on the bench and tried to concentrate on the game. But it wasn't easy to do with a strange, hairy leg. I tried to take deep breaths to calm myself down. Finally I was able to convince myself that I was imagining things.

In the meantime, the game was turning into a defensive battle, and it wasn't long before I was called upon to punt again. I saw the familiar shape of Coach walking down the sideline toward me. He was tall, broad shouldered, and, as always, wearing a sweatshirt and a Bulldogs baseball cap. He smiled at me.

"Fourth an ape," he said.

I felt a sudden rush of horror. Coach obviously had seen my hairy leg and now he was calling me out, saying that I was one-fourth an ape. Oh, this was a messy, messy situation.

"This ape thing Coach," I said, straining to keep calm, "it's a long story." But my nerves got the best of me and I began to ramble. "I guess if one of my legs is an ape leg, then approximately one-fourth of my weight is gorilla weight, so maybe I'm one-fourth an ape. Like you said. And you're wondering how I got to this way…well…. it's a long story…."

"I'm sure it is," interrupted Coach. "And after the game I might even ask you what the heck you are talking about. But, right now, it's *fourth and eight* and I need you to go in there and punt."

When I realized that Coach had said fourth *and eight*, not fourth *an ape*, I felt like the biggest dork on the planet, like king of the goofballs. But I also felt an all-encompassing sense of relief, as if I were 100 pounds lighter, almost like I could fly. I was downright giddy.

Thinking that I needed to say something, I continued to ramble, but it was a much happier ramble. "Fourth and eight? Ha, ha!" I laughed loudly. "Oh, I thought you said, fourth an, well, nevermind…" I stopped myself and stood there blushing.

Coach looked at me strangely. In another situation, he might ask me why I was acting so crazy, but there was a game of the field and he was trying to concentrate on it. He pointed me towards the field.

"Aim for the end zone, not the clouds," he said, slapping me on the back. "You can do it."

"You got it," I said, still elated that my secret had not been discovered.

As I jogged onto the field my leg felt good and strong, but it also felt unfamiliar. It was like driving someone else's sports car.

I stood 12 yards behind center, waiting for the ball to be snapped.

"Hut, hut, hut, HUT," I shouted and lifted my right leg. It was a fine snap, landing in my hands chest-high. One step, two steps, and PUNT! My leg swung upward. It felt strong and swift and made solid contact with the ball. WHAP! You could probably have heard the sound in the stands. I saw the ball soaring high *and* long.

Downfield, the punt returner looked to the sky and backpedaled a few steps. The ball sailed over his head. He turned around and dashed after it. Finally, he grabbed the ball at the four-yard line, but our players were all over him. He was tackled immediately. I jogged off the field. As I did, I looked up at our bench and saw about seven or eight players standing silently with their mouths agape. Suddenly they broke into cheers. "Wooooo baby, what a kick. Way to go Ivan!"

Some of the players were just laughing with amazement and glee. They obviously were having trouble believing their own eyes.

"Wow! Monster kick," said Zeph, shaking his head in disbelief as he ran onto the field. With 45-yard punts and monkeys stealing hats, I couldn't say that I blamed him.

I sat down on the bench next to Rensler, our left guard. He gave me a fist bump. "That was incredible," he said. "Keep up the good work, bro."

Toward the end of the first half, we scored a touchdown to bring the score to 14–13, with the Bearcats up by one point. I jogged onto the field and set up for the extra point. The snap was perfect. Mullen, our quarterback, jammed the ball into the turf and spun the laces. I booted it through the uprights for the extra point. Sure, I kicked it a bit harder than usual and the ball careened into the bleachers, but other than that there wasn't anything unusual about the play. Or so I thought. It turned out the referee threw a penalty flag. Apparently, the tight end was holding the defender.

We'd have to do the play over, except now—with the ten-yard penalty for holding—the ball was put at the 12-yard line. Now I'd need to either kick a 29-yard extra point or run a pass play to try and convert for two points. The longest I'd kicked in a game was a 25-yarder.

From the sidelines, Coach signaled for me to kick the extra point. The players took their positions. I lined up with the holder and took three steps backward and two steps to the left. When I kicked the ball, I heard the familiar THAP! only a bit louder than usual. I looked up and saw the ball sailing through the upper third of the goal posts and into the stands. The ref held his hands in the air: the kick was good and the score was tied at 14.

As I walked over to the bench, I saw Coach chuckling in amazement. "What the heck did you eat for breakfast?" he asked.

"Two bowls of oatmeal," I said.

"Eat that before every game." Coach laughed as he slapped me on the back.

Either the defenses were wearing down or the offenses were finally getting in synch, but I didn't need to punt very often in the second half. When I did, though, the kicks were boomers. There were two of them, and each traveled about 45 yards in the air. Each time the returner had to backpedal to field the ball; each time our bench erupted in cheers and laughter.

We battled back and forth with the Bearcats, exchanging touchdowns. Before I knew it, the score was even at 32 points. One minute remained in the game. We had the ball on our own 30-yard line.

We called a trick running play, trying to make big yardage, a delayed shovel pass to Tommy. He ran for 11 yards. On the next play our fullback was stopped at the line of scrimmage. On third down, the quarterback hit Tommy with a screen pass. He dodged one defender, and the blockers picked up two other defenders. It appeared that he had a clear shot at the end zone, but the Bearcat safety had the angle on him and tackled him at the 23-yard line.

There were seven seconds left on the clock. Coach called a time-out, and the team ran over to the sidelines. I usually wasn't a part of these huddles, but as I looked over I saw Coach signaling me to come over. Surprised, I jogged over to the huddle. I heard Tommy talking as I walked into the group of offensive players.

"Let me run it in," said Tommy. "I know I can do it."

"No, there's not enough time to do that," said Coach. "If you don't make it, we won't have time for another play."

"I know I can do it, Coach. Just let me have the ball."

"No, no," said Coach, shaking his head. "There's not enough time. Ivan's going to kick it."

Every head in the huddle suddenly turned and looked at me as if I had a totem pole growing out of my left shoulder. It wasn't hard to read their minds: "This is crazy. We never kick field goals. This is a high school game." I might have thought the same thing if I were them.

Finally Reggie broke the silence. "Good idea, Coach. He's been nailing the ball."

"Yeah, that's right," said right tackle Nate Sherman. "He's been booting it."

There was a general sense of agreement, with everyone nodding and mumbling affirmations. Everyone except Tommy, who looked annoyed and upset that he wasn't going to be called upon to carry the day. I could almost read his mind. "Hey, I ran the ball down to the 20. I deserve the call." But he knew that he couldn't say it aloud. That would sound too selfish and egotistical. Even for him.

There wasn't much time to think it over. Before I knew it, I was lined up behind Mullen, who was down on one knee and ready to take the snap. He turned and gave me the thumbs up. I paced off my five steps—three backward and two to the left— and prepared to kick the ball. It would be a 40-yard field goal; much farther than I had ever kicked in a game. But it was happening so fast and unexpectedly that I didn't even have time to get nervous.

"Forty-seven, 55, hut, hut, HUT!" I shouted. Reggie snapped the ball to Mullen. He quickly jammed the point of the ball into the ground and spun it so the laces faced away from me.

I ran a diagonal line at the ball, swung my leg, and BOOM! The contact felt clean and crisp. I glanced up and saw the ball fly end over end. Everything seemed to pass into slow motion. I watched the ball sail through the goalposts and into the stands.

The home crowd sat in stunned silence for a second or two. Then they went wild. The ball had landed in the lap of Mr. Wagner, my English teacher, whose hands had been occupied with a large soft drink and a bag of popcorn. The impact created an explosion of popcorn and soda. But in the melee that occurred afterward, even Mr. Wagner was seen jumping up and down, waving the game-winning football over his head. A few fans rushed onto the field, but the referees escorted them off. There were two seconds left on the clock.

I ran back onto the field for the kick-off. Brimming with confidence, I promptly booted it into the end zone. The Bearcat return man was stunned that the kick had traveled so far. With no time left on the clock, he had no choice but to run it out. He ran it to the five-yard line and was tackled by Zeph and Middlebury. Time ran out and the game was over. The drought had ended. We had finally beaten the Bearcats!

Now the fans, giddy with excitement and astonished by the uncharacteristic way in which the game had ended, rushed onto the field.

Coach was ecstatic, leaping up and down in a scrum of players. He grabbed me around the shoulders.

"Remember, two bowls of oatmeal for breakfast on game days," he shouted, and we all jumped up and down, cheering and high-fiving, all whoops and looks of happy disbelief.

12.

The celebration continued in the locker room. Dittmore and I were the heroes of the game.

"Good kick," Tommy said, lacking conviction.

"Good run. I couldn't have done it without you setting it up," I said, with only slightly more conviction. I wasn't going to concentrate on Tommy. I was thrilled with the victory and surprised by my starring role in it.

Coach brought in a bottle of sparkling cider, popped the cork, and poured it over Dittmore and me. It was a bit of overkill, but we hadn't beaten the Bearcats in ten years. I was so excited that I almost forgot about my leg. We exchanged stories about the game for a long time. Even the grunge of the locker room had a charming, homey glow that day.

Eventually, the players got dressed and trickled out of the building. I stayed behind. I was happy, but my denial was starting to wear off. I was beginning to have uneasy thoughts about being a boy with a gorilla leg.

What to do? Changing clothes in front of everyone was out of the question. If I had been shocked by my hairy leg, I couldn't imagine what everyone else would think.

So I waited them out. As the last player left the locker room, I relaxed a little bit, letting the tension in my shoulders dissipate. Suddenly Zeph barged through the door. I quickly pulled up my pants, nearly falling over in the process.

Then I did my best to act casual.

"Hi, Zeph," I said. "That was a great game, wasn't it?" This sounded obvious and somewhat idiotic, like saying, "Did you know that fish swim in water?" But I had to say something. As it was, Zeph just gave me a strange look and waved me toward the door.

"Hey, hurry up," said Zeph. "We're heading over to the Haven for dinner." The Haven was the preferred hangout for the football team, an inexpensive diner that served big portions at small prices. Many of the other students from Ellerbach liked to chow-down there, too.

"Great idea. How about I meet you there in about a half-hour?"

"No, let's go now. Get into your street clothes, and hurry up. You can ride in my car, and I'll give you a lift back to your car later. Everyone wants to know where you developed your new kicking skills."

"The supermarket," I said.

"The supermarket?" he exclaimed, bewildered. "You picked up your kicking skills at the supermarket? What are you talking about?" Zeph gave me another strange look. He seemed genuinely concerned about me.

"Oh, no. I mean I need to stop by the supermarket before I go to the Haven," I said, not sounding terribly convincing. "I've got to pick up something."

"C'mon, it can wait. We just beat the Bearcats, dude! Let's go celebrate. What's wrong with you?"

"Oh, nothing," I said, my mind searching for a good reason to go to the supermarket. "I just need to go by the drugstore and pick up some ointment for a rash. It's really bothering me. I wouldn't enjoy my meal."

"A rash?"

"Yeah, it's…you know." I signaled downward with my hands.

Zeph held up his hands. "That's okay. I don't want to know about your rash, and I don't want to know about Ipoo the monkey or any of your other crazy stories. Just hurry up and get to the Haven. We'll be waiting. *Hurry!*"

As soon as the door was closed, I made a quick survey of the locker room to make absolutely sure I was alone. I peered around each row of lockers and even checked inside the dismal showers. I slowly pulled down my football pants, not really wanting to see my right leg; but I knew that I'd have to look at it some time.

"Omigosh," I whispered as I stared at my leg. It wasn't a full-fledged gorilla leg, but it sure didn't look like *my* leg. Thin clusters of long black hair had darkened it. In other areas, there were clumps of shorter black hair. Then there were places without hair, but that didn't make it look any better. It looked like I had mange.

I opened my locker, pulled out my jeans and shirt, and put them on. I remembered what Dr. Carlson had told me about the top secret mission and how I was supposed to act normal. How absurd! What human could act normal with a gorilla leg? Maybe I shouldn't have been booting 45-yard punts and kicking 40-yard field goals. That was anything but normal and it certainly had drawn attention to me. But it was too late to change that now.

I sat on the bench, opened a Gatorade, took a swig, and contemplated my next move. A mouse stuck its head out from under a locker, its eyes looking like small, black beads. It darted to the middle of the floor, grabbed a crumb, and scrambled under the locker again.

I thought about the mice in Dr. Carlson's experiments. "They gave their last measure for science," Elko had said. I got a sinking feeling in my stomach and felt drops of perspiration beading up on my forehead. I hurriedly got dressed and walked outside, pulling out Dr. Carlson's business card and tapping his number into my cell phone.

"Veterinary hospital. Dr. Carlson speaking."

"Dr. Carlson, it's me," I said.

"Who's me?"

"It's Ivan."

"Ivan?"

"The kid who got jabbed with a needle in your lab last night," I blurted out, annoyed.

"Oh, yes, Ivan! You devil, you. How's everything going?" He sounded completely at ease, like he didn't have a care in the world.

"I'm not so sure. My leg is growing long, black gorilla hair."

There was silence on the other end of the telephone, a long penetrating silence.

"My leg seems to be getting more muscular, too," I continued. "It doesn't look like my leg anymore. I'm sure it's from the stuff that was in that syringe."

"How can that be? You only got a small dose, if you got any dose at all."

"My leg is getting bigger and it's growing long, black hair."

There was silence again on the other end of the phone. Obviously, the doctor was thinking.

"Well, this is fascinating for science, but not so good for you, I guess," he said, finally. "How do you feel?"

"I just kicked a 40-yard field goal."

"What?"

"I'm on the football team."

"Oh, well, that's fantastic. I mean it's good you're on the football team, getting exercise and all that. Hmmm." There was a long pause. I could almost see him on the other end, his finger rubbing his chin, his mind deep in thought. "Forty yards? Say, that's terrific," he continued. "Not too many 40-yarders in high school, are there?"

"It happens, but not very often," I said. "And this kick sailed through easily. I could have kicked it even farther."

Dr. Carlson was thinking on the other end of the line. "I might have to get a patent on these cross-species boosters that I've invented," he said breezily.

Here I sit with a gorilla leg, and he's thrilled about his discovery. I imagined the doctor smiling, staring off into space, pleased with himself, thinking of his scientific success.

"Hey, what about me? I have gorilla hair all over my leg!"

"Oh, yes, I was just getting to that," he stammered. "Elko will be in charge of that. I know he looks and acts like a bit of a beast, but he's a very good scientist. I would take this responsibility myself, but I need to visit our agents in the quarantine unit. You remember. I told you about all this."

"Can't I just come in now?"

"I'm at the airport right now. I'll try to coordinate with Elko while I'm gone. He's been privy to much of the research."

"Elko? He can't even control that monkey. He just sprayed it in the face with some sort of knockout gas."

"He invented that knockout gas. He's not just your run-of-the-mill scientist. He likes challenges. He'll work night and day on a cure for you."

"You've got to be kidding," I shouted, but Dr. Carlson quickly interrupted me.

"I've got to hop on the plane right now. I really don't think these gorilla attributes will last. Anyway, you won't be able to call me on this phone for a week. Elko will have my private number, if you really need it. I don't want to give it out over the phone. Let me give you Elko's number."

He gave me the number and hung up. I dialed the number but hung up before it rang, as I realized I didn't want to talk with Elko. I really didn't like the idea of my fate hanging with that guy.

What else could I do? I walked over to my beat-up car and drove to the Haven to celebrate the victory. And to tell you the truth, I forgot about my gorilla leg for a few hours and had a really good time.

13.

The next morning I called Elko.

"What's up, kid?"

"My left leg is turning into a gorilla leg. That's what's up."

"I know. I spoke with Dr. Carlson, and I saw your football game. You were amazing. Keep up the good work."

"You were at the football game?"

"Yeah, I love football."

"Did you see me punt and kick?

"I sure did. You were outstanding."

This struck me as a strange thing to say. Maybe he had watched the game because he was concerned about my health, or maybe he wanted to make sure that I didn't act strange and spill the beans about the secret research. It seemed strange that he was rooting for me.

"I punted the ball 40 yards. Doesn't that look suspicious?"

"Forty-five yards. And no, it looks terrific. I won 200 bucks on that game."

"What? You bet on high school football games? Isn't that a conflict of interest? What would Dr. Carlson say?"

"Never mind Dr. Carlson. You're working with me now. If you ever want to be normal again, just keep playing ball like you do."

"To do that, I need to keep my gorilla leg."

"Like I said, just keep playing like you did in the last game."

"What! You're going to let me run around with a gorilla leg?"

"Calm down, kid. You forget that I'm a scientist, too."

Elko chuckled. It seemed clear that he didn't have my best interests in mind, but he was my only connection to Dr. Carlson for the time being. I had to deal with him.

"So are you working on a cure, or is Dr. Carlson?" I huffed.

"We both are, so you'd better continue to be nice to me."

"Nice to you?" I said. *What a strange thing to hear from such a brute of a man,* I thought. "I didn't know that you were so sensitive."

"I meant that you better keep kicking field goals. That's how you're nice to Elko."

Okay, I thought, *so Elko wants me to keep kicking field goals. But to do that, I need the gorilla leg. And who knows where the gorilla-ness will stop. Maybe it will creep up to my stomach, my*

69

chest, and my neck! How will I look going to school with a
gorilla face?

Other disturbing thoughts followed. I imagined the
conversations that I'd have with the school secretary: "I'm sorry,
I won't be at school today. I feel okay, but I've developed *ape*
face. Don't be alarmed. It's not usual for me to come down with
it this time of year. I don't want to distract or frighten the other
students. I'll be back when my normal face returns."

I was absorbed in this downward spiral of disturbing thoughts
when Elko interrupted. "I know what you're thinking, kid.
You're wondering if this gorilla thing is going to stop at your leg.
Most likely it will. We've done quite a few experiments. You got
a very small dose."

"I hope you're right."

It made sense, but who really knew? We were in uncharted
territory. I figured if Elko wasn't concerned for my health, maybe
he was concerned for the top secret mission. Maybe a threat to
the mission would spur him into action.

"People are going to find out, Elko. My leg is getting big and
hairy."

"Go buy some baggy jeans. I'll even pay for them if you
keep kicking field goals like that."

"What about the gorilla hair all over my leg? People are bound to notice it. I mean, I can do my best to cover it up, but I won't be able to hide it for long."

"Yes, you will."

"How's that?"

"You're going to buy a razor today. Gillette sells nice ones. They're light green and they come in packages of five. You should probably shave your other leg, too, so they match. You don't want to draw attention to yourself."

I could hear Elko chortle. He really did find this amusing.

"Lots of fun for you," I said. "You're walking around with two human legs."

"That's what you get for sneaking into our laboratory." Elko chortled again.

He had a point. If I hadn't been wandering around the zoo after lights out, Ipoo wouldn't have stolen my cap and I wouldn't have gone looking for it in the veterinary hospital where I was accidentally injected with gorilla serum. But the penalty of a leg transformation was out of proportion with the crime. This was unfair punishment!

"I'm going to tell Dr. Carlson," I fumed.

"You don't have his number."

"C'mon, Elko. Give a kid a break."

"What do you mean? You're making history at Ellerbach High. You just continue doing what you're doing and I'll continue working on a cure."

I snorted into my cell phone in frustration, but there was no getting through to Elko. What choice did I have but to trust him? At least until Dr. Carlson got back into town.

"Alright, Elko. If I keep kicking and punting, you've got to stand up to your end of the bargain."

"Right, kid." Elko paused for a moment as if he were mulling things over. Then I heard a loud crunching noise. It was the unmistakable sound of him biting into an apple. I was forced to listen to him chew for a second or two.

"I'm trusting you, Elko," I said.

He didn't say anything for a while. Maybe he was thinking. Maybe he was swallowing a mouthful of chewed apple. Finally, he piped up.

"Who knows, you might start to enjoy having a gorilla leg."

"Enjoy it? What are you talking about?

"You heard me."

He hung up the phone and I was left standing on the sidewalk in front of my house scratching my gorilla leg.

14.

In the next week, I tried to go about life in an ordinary fashion, as best I could. Some things were easier than others. A few things would require practice. One of the things I was dreading was buying women's razors at the drugstore. Not only was it embarrassing, but it was concrete evidence that I had a gorilla leg that needed to be shaved. I guess I could have just bought a men's razor, but I wasn't sure if they were good for shaving legs. Red-faced, I brought a package of razors up to the counter.

"It's for my sister," I told the clerk.

"I thought your sister was eight," said the clerk. I looked up at the clerk and suddenly realized that he was a friend of my parents. I shouldn't have said anything.

"I'm sorry. It's for my aunt. She's in France."

"France?"

"Yes, near Spain. Spanish France."

"Spanish France?"

"Or thereabouts," I said, blushing and looking down at the chewing gum displays below the cash register and considering cramming a bunch of pieces into my mouth so I wouldn't have to answer any more questions. The clerk dug for change in the register drawer, humming to himself. He was taking forever.

"Here you go." Handing me my change, the clerk looked me over once more. I felt my face getting redder. Then slowly his expression changed. He pointed his finger at me like a pistol. "Hey, great kicking the other night." A smile broadened over his face. "That was a monster of a kick. A game-winner."

"Oh, thanks. Thanks a lot," I said, a bit surprised.

"Keep up the good work."

"I'll try to."

I walked out the door with a five-pack of razors, a notebook, and a package of gummy bears. I smiled to myself, happy to be acknowledged for my game-winning field goal. But I also realized that I would need to do a better job getting my story straight.

15.

During football practice, Coach took a new interest in me. I practiced field goals and extra points, with him looking on. He was making me nervous. I kept checking my football pants to make sure they were pulled down to cover my bulging calf.

"Why didn't I notice this before?" asked Coach. "You're a powerful kicker."

"Well, the Bulldogs never had much of a kicking game before," I said. "So I really didn't get to show my stuff." Coach was quiet for a moment as he mulled this over. He scratched the side of his head.

"I never really practiced that hard until a couple of months ago," I said. "Plus, I've been lifting a lot of weights."

Coach nodded his head, accepting this explanation. "This adds a new dimension to our offense. You and Tommy Dittmore."

Ugh, that guy again! Dittmore was a pain in my neck. He didn't share everyone else's enthusiasm for my kicking. In fact, he didn't like to share much of anything, least of all the limelight. I remembered that whiff of resentment from him in the aftermath of the Bearcats game. But he was our best halfback, and we were on the same team. We needed to pull together.

Coach watched me kick for about 40 minutes, as I booted one after another through the uprights. I had always been an accurate kicker, so the new-found power was a big boost to my game. Of course, it's harder to kick a long field goal accurately. Maintaining precision with the increased power for kicking long distances was a challenge. But the more I practiced, the better I got.

"Amazing," Coach said. "Keep eating that oatmeal for breakfast."

I really hadn't intended to be the team's kicker. I'd wanted to be the tight end, but my size and speed were not quite up to par with the first-string players. Besides, I had showed an aptitude for the kicking game. That's how I came to be the team's punter and kicker.

Generally, players come into the positions differently. Most, I guess, would choose to be either a kicker or a punter—one or the other. It's rare that a player would have both skills, but our team didn't have a lot of talent in those positions. And I loved doing it.

It was a chance to play on the first string and contribute to the team.

What I liked best was the feeling and the sound of my foot hitting the ball in perfect stride, kicking the ball in the sweet spot, hearing the *thwap* of my foot connecting with the leather, and feeling in my bones that it had been a good kick. Sometimes when I kicked it just right, I just knew it was sailing through the uprights. That was a great feeling.

I kicked soccer style, wearing a soccer shoe on one foot and a football cleat on the other. The soccer shoe fit tighter than the football cleat, giving me added control and more foot feel. The football cleat on my non-kicking foot really dug into the ground, giving me stability when I kicked or punted the ball.

Unlike placekicking, punting is a defensive strategy. But just like placekicking, punting gave me a glorious feeling when I really connected with the ball. Punting has many elements, but two of the most important are distance and hang time.

The punts I liked best were the ones where we were near our own 20-yard line. I had the freedom to get my foot on the ball and go for a long, booming punt with lots of hang time. There's nothing like the feeling of connecting with the ball and sending it high and long and getting your team out of trouble. I loved getting the job done, and the team always appreciated it.

How did the gorilla leg work in all of this? I'll be frank. Pretty darn well! The funny thing is that the gorilla leg was more powerful *and* more accurate. It seemed to have an innate sense of coordination; I got the feeling that if you could train a gorilla to kick, you could have a high-scoring offense.

Of course, there's one last thing: while it certainly was fun to boot the heck out of the ball and help the team, I still worried about turning into a gorilla. It had only been a few days and there was no telling where the gorilla-ness might end. And keeping the leg undercover was going to get harder and harder.

16.

I was well rested for the next game. Although my leg felt stronger than ever before, there hadn't been any changes to the rest of my body—at least none that I noticed.

We were playing the Roosevelt Panthers, a very good team from south of the city. We hadn't beaten them in years, and they looked like they might win their division this year.

We took the field, doing the usual stretches and half-speed plays. The defensive players banged on each other's shoulder pads and loosened up. As game time neared we ran to the sidelines and gave the team cheer.

"Go, Bulldogs!"

They kicked off. The game had begun.

There was no defensive struggle; it was a high scoring game. Tommy Dittmore had a couple of big runs, and our fullback Andy Castro made a sensational catch—I think it was the first pass he ever caught in a game, and it just happened to be in the end zone. Right on, Andy!

I kicked the extra point. The kick felt smooth and sure-footed, like the workings of a clock.

I also kicked a nice 38-yarder straight through the uprights. It was a thing of beauty. Mr. Wagner was ready for it this time: no soda or popcorn in hand. He tried to catch the ball, but it sailed a few feet over his head. He looked a little disappointed that he didn't get to make the play. He'd get another chance.

The next drive we were stopped at the 30-yard line. I nailed a 47-yard field goal, and we won the game 23–14. I had kicked three field goals and two extra points.

I looked into the end zone. It was a bedlam of cheering, shouting, and pom-pom waving. Mr. Wagner was holding up the ball from my final kick, and all the students were clustering around him shouting, "We're number one!" Of course, we weren't number one yet, but the fact that we were a winning team was astonishing to most of our fans, and to be honest, most of our players, too.

Students were starting to get excited about our football team. A good deal of the enthusiasm was created by my kicking. To everyone who watched, I seemed to have come out of nowhere to suddenly boot 47-yard field goals. To tell you the truth, I reveled a bit in the glory.

But off the field, I had my concerns. I worried about turning into a gorilla. I fretted about catching some incurable gorilla disease. Most of all, I worried about the mice in Dr. Carlson's experiments that died before becoming gorilla-mice. I wondered if my body could support gorilla changes that might be moving upward from my leg.

Some of the changes were dietary. I noticed a craving for waffles. Yes, waffles. Every morning I wolfed down eight frozen waffles with butter and maple syrup. (I didn't give in to Coach's superstition of eating two bowls of oatmeal before games.)

I ate food that I'd never liked before, such as kale. I could eat a whole bundle of kale straight out of the refrigerator. A green and bitter leaf, kale was not the kind of food I'd ever eaten before. No one else in my family had either. But Mom bought it one day just to try it, and after that I kept asking her to put it on the shopping list. Although this urge worried me in some ways, I was glad for it in other ways. A pound of kale a day would give me the vitamins and fiber that were not supplied by waffles, butter, and maple syrup. Waffles were the yin and kale was the yang. My family just thought I was practicing extra hard at football and needed the calories and vitamins.

I wanted bananas too, but I tried to keep myself from eating too many of them. Too monkey-like. One day when I was

81

mulling over whether I should eat another banana, I had an idea. Maybe if I embraced my gorilla-ness, I could convince Elko that I was transforming into a gorilla. Then he would work harder at finding a cure.

I didn't imagine for a minute that Elko would feel sorry for me. That simply wasn't in his nature. But there was no way a full-fledged gorilla would be allowed to play football—or even be in school. The jig would be up!

As you might imagine, since my fateful accident I had read a lot about gorillas. But now I was devouring the subject matter with a new intensity. I studied videos of gorillas, watching the way they walked, grunted, scratched, hooted, and hollered. I watched them as they ate their meals and groomed one another. I learned their various vocalizations.

When no one was around to hear me, I acted out the parts. I was a large silverback beating on my chest. I was a teenage gorilla, searching for a troop to join. I was an adult gorilla, foraging through the forest. I was King Kong. I was a method actor of gorilla-ness.

Finally, after three days I was ready. I performed my breathing exercises, stretched my limbs, picked up the phone and tapped in Elko's number, prepared to convince him that I had changed into a full-fledged gorilla.

After three rings, he picked up. He always let it ring three times.

"Hello," he said.

"Mush, mush, mango, it's Iiiiivannn," I said in my best half-human, half-gorilla voice. "Mango, mango, maaaanngoooo."

"Who is this?"

"Mush, mango, it's Iiiiivannn, mush, mush."

I heard a loud shriek on the other end of the phone. A bone-chilling shriek of horror! I had done it! I was no longer Ivan the football player. I was Ivan the gorilla, at least to Elko. Now he was aghast by the ugly turn of events and, quite frankly, he deserved it. The callous swine! He might even feel responsible. Perhaps I had misjudged him. Maybe he had a heart after all.

"Mango, maaaanngoooo, I hope it's not too late for me, mush, mush!" I said emphatically. I was really pouring it on. I was hamming it up. If there were an Oscar for animal imitations, I would have gone home with a shiny statuette in my hand.

There was another loud shriek on the other end of the phone. But this one sounded a little different. There was a little wackiness in it. Suddenly, I realized that these weren't shrieks of horror that I had been hearing. They were shrieks of *laughter*. He was laughing at me! Now I could really hear the familiar chortling.

"Oh, my, that's rich! I've got to see you do that in person. Ho-ho, har-har," he howled. I could actually hear him slapping his big hand on his giant thigh.

"I'm turning into a gorilla, Elko."

"Ha, nice try, kid."

"Don't you have any compassion?"

"I do. I feel sorry for you. That was the lamest gorilla imitation I've ever heard."

I was more than a little miffed at this. Not only was he insensitive to my plight, now he was insulting my acting.

"What are you talking about?" I seethed. "If a gorilla could speak English, that's exactly how he would sound. What do you know anyway?"

"I know a lot. That sounded like someone with their face squeezed in an elevator door."

"It sounded like a cross between a gorilla and a human!" I insisted.

"No way. Wrong tone. Wrong inflection. Listen to this," he said. There was a long pause. I waited impatiently, tapping my foot. Suddenly, through the phone, I heard an ear-shattering roar, a horrible combination of a deep bellow and the wildest banshee scream I'd ever heard. Instinctively, my hands flew up and the phone sailed into the air.

I shook the lingering sensation out of my ear and picked up the phone. "What the heck was that?"

"It's my silverback war cry. Pretty impressive, eh?"

"It's horrendous."

"Just a second…"

He let out another blood-curdling scream and the phone nearly flew out of my hands again. The hair was standing up on the back of my neck.

"If you ever want to change the school mascot to a gorilla, I could be paid to do that," said Elko. "Anyway, that's what a human gorilla would sound like when he's going off to battle. Sort of a scream and a roar at the same time. I could teach you if you'd like."

"That's okay. It's your specialty not mine."

"Suit yourself."

"Why is it called a silverback *war* cry? Gorillas aren't really warlike; they're actually quite peaceful."

"Did it sound peaceful to you? Maybe you should hear it again?" said Elko.

"No!" I shouted.

"Are you sure?"

"Yes!"

"Alright then. So what are our chances against Castlemoor High this weekend? I know it's an away game."

"I can't believe you."

"What?"

"I'm sitting here with a gorilla leg and you want to talk football."

"C'mon, I demonstrated my silverback war cry for you. The least you can do is give me your thoughts on the upcoming game."

I let out a sigh. It was futile to argue with him.

"Well, they usually beat us," I said. "But between Dittmore and myself, I'd say we've got a decent chance. They're a tough opponent, but we're playing well."

He took a minute to digest this. Or maybe he was filling out his betting card.

"How many points?" he asked.

"What?"

"How many points will we win by, if you had to guess?"

"Geez, Elko, how should I know? We haven't played them since last year, and they beat the pants off us in that game."

"But things are different this year."

"Yes, things are different this year. Especially for me."

"Hmmm," he said, mulling it over.

"Don't you even care about me turning into a gorilla?"

"Listen, kid," he said flatly. "I do worry about you turning into a gorilla. I'm doing the best I can. And so is Dr. Carlson. Just endure this until the end of the season, okay? I'll buy you a bunch of bananas. Organic ones." He burst out laughing again.

"End of the season?" I shouted. "How about when you find a cure? That should be soon, right? Aren't you working on a cure?"

"Of course I am, kid."

"So why do I have to wait for the end of the season? So you can make a few bucks off me?"

"No, the end of the season corresponds to the time that Dr. Carlson comes back, hopefully with…" He paused for a moment. "Most *assuredly* with a cure."

"I thought you were helping him."

"I am helping him. We're both working on it."

"Why didn't you go with him? Are you staying behind to watch me?"

"To some degree. If anything takes a turn for the worse, I can report it to the doctor. Also, I'm here to make sure that you continue acting as if nothing is wrong. We want to keep this secret."

"How is my kicking a 45-yard field goal keeping it a secret?"

"Stop trying to complicate things, kid. We've been over this before. The better you play, the harder I work."

Crunch! He was eating an apple again. I could hear the chomping on the other end of the phone.

"And besides, I think if you'd let yourself you might even enjoy this."

"Really?"

"Yes, really," he said.

"What makes you think that?"

"Because kicking field goals is fun," Elko said. "Now go out there and win one for the Gipper!"

17.

The game against the Castlemoor Eagles was an important one. If we beat Castlemoor, our confidence would soar. They had shut us down in our last two games, holding us to just seven points in each matchup. This was a chance to prove that we were a completely different team.

We felt loose as we took the field during warm-ups. But that didn't mean we were taking anything for granted. We expected a tough contest.

The game began auspiciously, with me booting the ball into the end zone. As I jogged over to the bench, I heard cheers from the crowd. I looked up at the stands. They were full! In the three years I'd been at Ellerbach, I'd never seen so many fans. It was a good feeling.

I looked over at Coach. He was as relaxed as I'd ever seen him. With Dittmore running the ball, Mullen throwing short passes, and me kicking field goals, we had developed a potent offense. Our defense was solid, especially with Zeph holding down the position of middle linebacker. Put it all together and we had amassed the best seasons in memory. But it wasn't over yet.

On their first offensive drive, the Eagles were stopped at the 50-yard line and had to punt. After a short runback, we started from our own 15-yard line, but we were moving the ball fairly well. We converted for a series of first downs, but were stopped at the 45-yard line on a third-down-and-three play.

"Ivan, get in there and boot it through the uprights," said Coach.

The Eagles were surprised that we'd even consider a field goal from that distance. It would be a 62-yard attempt! They called a time-out to bring in a few new players. Maybe they thought the kick would be a fake.

"Fourteen, 35, blue mongoose, hut, hut, HUT!" I yelled and stomped my foot. Reggie snapped the ball. Mullen caught it, and with one continuous motion stuck the pointed end into the turf and spun the laces.

I bounded toward the ball and BOOM! It went sailing straight through the middle of the goal posts. I could hear the crowd cheering, but most of all I could hear Coach.

"What a boot!" said Coach, laughing with glee and bounding up and down. "Ha ha, what a super boot! Good job, Super Booter!"

The players on the bench laughed. Then they chimed in.

"Way to go, Super Booter!"

"Super Booter, yeah!"

It was a seminal moment. The players, loving a good nickname, kept shouting it over and over, and it wasn't long before the crowd picked up on it. From there it spread like a prairie fire, starting out in one section of the stands and then spreading to little pockets all over the stadium.

I thought it might be a one-time joke. But I heard a few shouts of "Super Booter" from the crowd when I teed up the ball to kick off. I heard it again when I punted. Still, I thought it might die down.

By the second half, thanks to a particularly rowdy group of students, it morphed into a cheer, with much of the student body participating. I lined up to kick a field goal and the stadium erupted.

"Super Booter, Super Booter, ooh, aah!"

At first, I was embarrassed by the attention. The good thing about football is that no one can see your face turn red inside a football helmet. By my third appearance on the field in the second half, I had grown comfortable with the cheer, and in fact, I was kind of enjoying it. Without thinking, I waved at the crowd while they were cheering. The crowd went wild. That sealed the deal. From that game forward, every time I ran onto the field I was destined to hear this cheer.

"Super Booter, Super Booter, ooh, aah!"

"Super Booter, Super Booter, ooh, aah!"

I might as well have had Super Booter written on the back of my jersey.

Did I like my new nickname? Well, it didn't matter. The crowd, players and even Coach seemed to love the name.

Okay, yes I admit to liking the name. Sure it was a little immodest, but I didn't choose it. The name was thrust upon me. And finally the crowd was having some fun at the games, which really motivated the players.

There was also another dilemma the nickname Super Booter solved. If you're named Ivan, eventually people will try to nickname you *Ivan the Terrible.* It's just natural. You could be the nicest person in the world, but if your name is Ivan, folks will eventually call you Ivan the Terrible.

I lived in mortal dread of being nicknamed Ivan the Terrible. Don't get me wrong. It's an outstanding nickname for a defensive end or a linebacker. Any linebacker worth his salt would love to be called Ivan the Terrible.

But it's a horrible name for a field-goal kicker. It sounds like you're a clod who duffs most of his field goal attempts.

In fact, before the advent of Super Booter, I fantasized about being our starting wide receiver. I dreamed of trading names with Zeph so I could be called *The Zephyr,* the split end that could sprint downfield, pull in fingertip catches, and confidently stride into the end zone like a cool breeze. Of course, Zeph would be renamed Ivan, so he could be called *Ivan the Terrible,* the bone-crushing middle linebacker, the bane of running backs throughout the region. One can dream, right?

Well, that never happened. But Super Booter did. And because I liked it, I played it cool. Nothing ruins a nickname faster than letting everyone know you like it.

I made a lot of appearances in the first half, kicking off, punting, and kicking extra points, not to mention two field goals. Early in the third quarter, we scored a touchdown to tie the game at 27. I teed the ball up, prepared for the kickoff, and waited for the Super Booter cheers to die down. I was about to take my first stride toward the ball when I noticed a small shape running on the field near the opponent's 30-yard line. The shape was making a beeline for the football. Suddenly I got a queasy feeling, the same feeling I'd had at the zoo when I saw that unknown animal running at me. And for good reason. Once again, before I could react, Ipoo the demon monkey had arrived. This time he grabbed the football and ran toward our sideline.

It took a moment or two for the referee to believe what had happened. Then he blew his whistle and charged after the monkey. The Bulldogs jumped from the bench and dashed onto the gridiron, trying to stop Ipoo from fleeing with the ball. Seeing the mass of players coming toward him, Ipoo pivoted and ran toward Castlemoor's sideline. As he neared it, the entire Eagles team leapt to their feet and began chasing the evasive monkey. Ipoo pivoted again, this time dashing toward the goalpost as if he was trying to score a touchdown.

Ipoo would have made a terrific halfback. He was quick and low to the ground. As a player would near him, he would dart at the last instant, escaping their grasp. But Ipoo could only last so long, carrying the football. After all, he was a macaque, an animal used to running on all fours. And the football was about a third of his size.

Eventually, he dropped the football. But Ipoo wouldn't leave the field.

The crowd roared with laughter as the players, coaches, and referees chased the monkey around the field. Finally, from the stands a large man dressed in black walked onto the field with a small rectangular object in his extended right hand. In an instant, I recognized the scene. It was Elko, holding an ice cream sandwich. Sensing the determination in Elko's stride, the players and the referees parted down the middle like the Red Sea. The raucous crowd was suddenly silent as they watched the scene unfolding on the field.

Elko approached the tentative monkey standing on the 40-yard line. He extended his hand with the ice cream sandwich. The crowd watched intently.

As Ipoo slowly reached for the sandwich, Elko's other arm flashed out from behind his back in an instant. *Psssssst!* He blasted Ipoo with three seconds of spray from an aerosol can. Ipoo stood up straight, stunned. Then he took six or seven jittery steps and fell face first onto the field.

The crowd erupted. "Booooooo!"

Elko hurriedly grabbed Ipoo, tucked him under his arm like a stuffed animal, and walked toward the exit. Cups, cans, and assorted garbage hailed down from the stands, landing on the field. Elko, ever the charmer, made a nasty gesture at the crowd.

"Booooooo!" More garbage landed on the field as Elko grumpily strode to the exit with Ipoo under his arm.

The game did not start back up right away; it couldn't. For one thing, all the trash on the field needed to be picked up. For another, the referees and the security officials were conferring on the sidelines. Officials with walkie-talkies yammered on and on about who-knows-what while the crowd grew noisy and restless.

Men and women in solid black security outfits or black-and-white referee shirts scratched their heads, rubbed their chins, and shifted from leg to leg, trying to decide what to do next. Apparently, very little was written in the rulebook about how to officiate an instance of *ball theft by monkey prior to kickoff.*

Finally, the Bulldog marching band was sent onto the field to pick up the trash. After about five minutes, the amplified sound of someone tapping the microphone in the announcer's booth came over the loud speaker.

"Football fans, we have an update," said the deep-voiced announcer. "We've spoken to the man who took the monkey from the field. He has told us that the spray is harmless, and when the monkey wakes up in the next few hours, he will be given the ice cream sandwich."

Scattered cheers came from the crowd, slowly increasing to a round of hearty applause, then a crescendo of cheering and stomping.

"Ice cream, ice cream, oooh, aaah!" shouted the crowd. "Ice cream, ice cream, oooh, aaah!"

Sensing that things were getting a little too rowdy, the referee blew the whistle and signaled to our bench that it was time to kick off. The band was rushed off the field, trash bags in hand.

Once the band was off the field, the players jogged onto the field in preparation for the kickoff. "Super Booter, Super Booter, ooh, aah!" shouted the crowd. It was almost deafening.

I placed the ball on the tee and trotted back ten steps. I raised my hand, paused for a moment to look at the team. Then I bounded forward in a strong, controlled manner and booted the ball to the back of the end zone.

We were back to playing football.

It was a difficult and seesawing game with the lead changing three times in the second half. But I kicked two field goals in the fourth quarter, and we won the game by four points. Go Bulldogs!

18.

The Bulldogs were playing like a well-oiled machine. We won our next three games against Broomfield, Campton and Meridian. Football fever had hit Ellerbach High. I continued to hit long-range field goals, just as I continued to nag Elko about finding an antidote.

We took it easy during the following week because our opponents, the Belmont Cougars, were not a good team. We practiced, of course, but we rested more than usual. Maintaining balance is important, to prevent injury.

The easy practices were a welcome respite. I was able to concentrate on my schoolwork, and my social life, which that had taken a turn for the better since the advent of Super Booter.

At first I was slightly uncomfortable with high school fame and popularity, and I kept close to my old friends. However, I soon began to accept my good fortune.

The Super Booter cheer evolved, too. There was even a small article on it, on the Bulldogs football blog:

How to Do the Super Booter Cheer

Fans, here's how to get the most out of the Super Booter cheer: extend your thumbs out and point your index fingers to the sky, making an "L" with one hand and a backwards "L" with the other. Bring the tips of the thumbs together to make a goalpost. Put the goalpost in front of your face. Now say, "Super Booter, Super Booter, ooh, aah!" With the "ooh," fully extend your goalposts forward, like you're pushing out the slide of a trombone. Now bring the goalposts back in front of your face with the "aah." Repeat. After a few times, you'll find yourself really enjoying it.

Be careful, it's addictive!

I feigned embarrassment whenever I heard the Super Booter cheer in the halls of the high school, but after a while it seemed only noble to acknowledge the cheer with good-hearted wave or a wink. I was often regaled with it as I walked between classes, or on the bus. If I drove to school, sometimes if I was stopped at a stoplight and other Ellerbach students were in the car beside me, they might just mouth out, "Ooh, aah," to me—a kind of Super Booter shorthand.

One day I heard the Super Booter cheer as I was walking down the hallway at school. I turned to see a group of giggling freshmen girls. I did the Super Booter cheer back to them, only changing the words. "Cute girls, cute girls, oooh, aah," I said and smiled. They turned red and giggled again. I tipped my baseball cap to them. So young and free, so much to learn, what did they know about life?

You might think that I was getting caught up in Super Booter mania. I wasn't. Alright, maybe a *little* bit. But you have to understand, this was all thrust upon me. I had little say in the matter.

And then, before I knew it, the loveliest girl in the entire school, Kipper Swanson, and I were dating. Okay, we'd been on one date. But this was a big deal. And we seemed to click. She was an athlete herself, a star swimmer. We loved the same things in life.

Kipper and I were the King and Queen for the Old Gold parade, which was like a homecoming parade. In previous years, the parade was poorly attended because the team wasn't all that good. But this year attendance couldn't have been better. Kipper and I sat on top of the Old Gold float, wearing our illustrious crowns, listening to the band, and waving to the crowd. Suddenly, the band stopped playing and we could hear the cheer.

"Super Booter, Super Booter, ooh, aah," shouted the crowd as we passed.

"Super Booter, Super Booter, ooh, aah," they shouted again as though they wanted something more.

"Look, Kipper," I said. "They want us to do the Super Booter cheer." We were in no position to deny the crowd, so we obliged them with the cheer. And when we finished the cheer, we briefly kissed each other through our Super Booter goalposts.

My parents were mortified, but the crowd went nuts.

19.

The gorilla leg supplied the power, but I still needed to practice. The team was depending on my kicking more and more. Coach had written me into the offensive plan. Every day I would stop by my house, change into my practice gear, and drive to the field for football practice. I would do calisthenics with the team for half an hour and then run a few laps around the goalposts. Three days a week, I did strengthening exercises, usually in the weight room in the stadium. Or the team would bring the free weights onto the field, and we'd work out there.

I practiced my field goals and punts, and my leg never seemed to get tired. I had seven balls dedicated to me for practice. But after I'd kicked or punted the balls, I'd have to fetch them. Sometimes the team manager or water boy would retrieve the balls for me, but most days I was on my own. Sure, it was good exercise, but I thought the time would be better spent kicking that ball than retrieving it.

One day, after practice, I was sitting around the house trying to do my homework when I got an idea. I hopped into my car and drove toward the zoo. I had a favor to ask, and I thought I should ask Elko in person.

I flashed the membership card Dr. Carlson had given me at the gate and strolled through the zoo to the veterinary hospital. When I walked into the lab, I saw Elko sitting with his feet up on the desk. His chair looked tiny in contrast to his enormous body. He was reading from a notebook and next to him was a can of soda, a bag of chips, and several magazines.

"Is this what you do when Dr. Carlson isn't around?" I asked. I thought he'd be surprised to see me, but he just glanced over.

"No, usually I don't come in at all when Dr. Carlson's isn't around," he said drily, as he took a pen from the desk and scribbled something into his notebook. I assumed he was kidding. Actually, Elko struck me as a hardworking sort of guy. Hardworking at *what* was the question.

"Are those the notes for the cure for the gorilla leg? You know, the cure you're working on night and day?"

"No, this is a poem. I've been writing a poem."

"A poem? I didn't take you as the poetic type. What kind of poem are you writing?"

"It's about a guy who is visited by a big crow. The bird keeps squawking 'Nevermore,' and it drives the man crazy. His girlfriend's name is Eleanor, so it rhymes with nevermore. By the way, Eleanor is dead and the crow knows it."

"That sounds familiar," I said.

"You must have seen it on my website," said Elko. "I posted it there about a week ago. But I'm making a few changes to it now."

"Elko, that poem has already been written. It's called 'The Raven,' and it was written by Edgar Allen Poe."

Elko stared at me for a moment, as if he wasn't sure what I was talking about. Then he burst out, "What? Someone stole my poem? I knew I shouldn't have put it on my website. Why, who is this Edward Poe guy? I'll crush him into a ball!" He slammed his open palm on top of the empty soda can, crushing it flat.

"His name is Edgar Allan Poe, and you'll have an easy time crushing him into a ball. He's been dead for 150 years."

Elko threw down his pen and grunted again. "What?"

"We learned about him in English class. He lived in Baltimore, married his cousin, and liked to write spooky stories."

"Well, he was ahead of his time," said Elko, finally.

"Because he married his cousin?"

104

"No, not for that," shouted Elko. "Because he wrote stories about sinister birds."

"Let me see that." I grabbed the poem off his desk and looked at the first few stanzas. "The only things that are different are that you changed the raven into a crow and you changed the girlfriend's name from Lenore to Eleanor."

Elko got grumpy and dismissive. "Ah, whatever, I've got a better story I'm working on."

"I'd like to hear about that story someday, but I came to ask you a favor."

"A favor? I charge between 50 to 100 bucks for favors," he said. "What's the favor?"

I assumed he was kidding, so I went ahead. "Alright, so I've been practicing my kicking every day. I have seven footballs that I kick and punt. The problem is that I need someone to fetch them after I kick them. The team manager and the water boy are getting sick of doing it, so most days I have to retrieve them. So I was wondering if I could borrow Ipoo to fetch the balls. He seems to like doing it. Remember that day he ran out during halftime and stole the ball?"

"How could I forget? The crowd booed me until I left the stadium."

"Well, what do you think? Could I borrow him? Would he do it?"

"He'd love to do it. It certainly would be a lot better for him than being cooped up around here." Elko paused for a moment, scratching the side of his face. "It's just the matter of the cost."

"The cost? Don't tell me you're going to charge me."

"No, *I'm* not going to charge you. *Ipoo* is going to charge you."

"What does Ipoo charge?"

"If I know Ipoo, I figure it will cost you about five ice cream sandwiches a week to keep him motivated."

"Deal," I said.

And so every day before practice I showed up at the lab and took Ipoo over to the stadium. After, I'd stop by the Quick Mart and buy an ice cream sandwich that Ipoo would eat on his way back to the laboratory. Elko was glad that Ipoo was getting some outdoor time, and I was happy that I had a football retriever. The players were delighted with their new mascot, even though we kept the name Bulldogs.

The Macaques or the Ipoos didn't sound quite right for a football team.

20.

Saturday's opponent was the Madison Cougars, a team that we had beaten the year before, when our record wasn't all that good. However, we weren't taking any games for granted. We were determined to go out and play our best.

I had a little trouble with my accuracy during the first half, missing a 58-yard field goal, but no one held that against me. I got my groove back on my next field goal attempt, a 54-yarder. I continued to kick field goals throughout the game, and the score stood at 41–14 when the final seconds ticked off the clock.

While most of the game was unremarkable, one interesting thing did happen near the end of the first half. I was about to punt, standing ten yards in the backfield, waiting for the snap. The blocking assignments were simple. The offensive line would block the defensive line. Tommy and Andy Castro stood several yards in front of me to block any defenders who made it around the offensive line. The Cougars, frustrated with my long punts, sent an extra man on a blitz to attempt to block the punt. It shouldn't have been a problem, but Tommy missed his man, and I needed to rush my punt to keep it from being blocked.

Here's the thing: I am being generous by saying that Tommy "missed" his blocking assignment. From where I was standing, it looked like he brushed past the defender, barely making contact, and ran downfield.

As I was walking toward the bench, I made eye contact with him, trying to get a response from him about the missed block. He glanced at me, gave me the usual half-smile-half-sneer, and looked away.

Anyone can miss a blocking assignment, right? But it happened again in the second half. Tommy brushed by his man and ran downfield, making me hurry my punt. Once again, when I looked at him I received the same half-smile-half-sneer.

I couldn't stand it. I liked talking with Tommy about as much as I liked dental surgery, but he'd pushed me too far. If he was purposely missing his blocking assignment to get at me, it was a low-down, ugly trick. And I couldn't go into future games wondering if Tommy was going to sandbag me like that. In the locker room, I approached him.

"You missed your blocking assignments on two punts," I said.

"Yeah, so what?" he grumbled, not looking at me.

"You're a better player than that."

He stood up. "What are you trying to say, that I missed my assignment on purpose?"

Whoa! A little hasty to take offense. Methinks he protests too much, I thought.

"I'm not saying anything. I'm just asking," I said.

"Who are you to ask me? You're just the kicker." He was really steamed, yelling at me. I was starting to get agitated, too.

"I punt, too," I said, my voice getting louder. "And I don't like the idea of getting knocked on my butt when it's not necessary. This is a team game, you know."

Now other players were standing up, walking over.

"That's right," Tommy said. "It is a team game. But ever since you started making a contribution, it's all about you."

"Well, if that isn't the pot calling the kettle black, I don't know what is."

"What's that supposed to mean?"

"Knock it off, Tommy," said the fullback, Andy Castro, stepping in front of Tommy. "You're way out of line." This really made Tommy seethe, because if anyone else might have noticed the missed blocks, it was the big fullback.

"Fine," said Tommy, flinging up his arms and turning toward the gathering of players. "But let me tell you this. There's something fishy about that guy. No one just starts kicking 60-yard field goals. And I'm going to get to the bottom of this. We used to be a team. And now look what's happening."

This, of course, was an incredibly stupid thing to say. Everyone was thrilled with what I was doing with the team, and with the team as a whole. We were playing very well and were enjoying success for once. If this was his attempt to rally the team against me, he had failed miserably. Everyone looked at him like he had lost his mind. The only thing he managed to do was underscore his complete lack of team spirit. And now Coach was walking over.

"I think you'd better go outside and do two laps around the goalposts," said Coach to Tommy.

Tommy backed up and sneered at me. He looked like he might come at me. But Castro raised one eyebrow, as if to say, "You're going to have to go through me to get to him."

Tommy turned abruptly and headed out the locker room door toward the field, but not before announcing to no one in particular, "I'll get to the bottom of this."

"Better make that three laps, Tommy," Coach said as Tommy walked out the locker room door.

21.

Tommy seemed to avoid me after that, basically because the team didn't support his outlandish behavior. But I was wary of Tommy's potential for behind-the-scenes maneuvering. I had heard that he'd been asking the other players if they'd noticed anything weird about me. Most of them only stated the obvious: that I had been punting and kicking remarkably well, like never before. Mostly, they tried to brush him off.

But I knew that if Tommy were to see my right foot after I took off my shoes and socks, he'd really have something real to go on. I was careful to keep my foot and leg shaved, just in case someone might see them. A new problem, however, was beginning to emerge. My foot was getting wider, and it looked as though my big toe might be separating from the rest of my foot, looking more like a thumb than a big toe. An unpleasant thought of me eating a banana with my foot popped into my head. Even though I knew gorillas can't grab things with their feet the way orangutans can, the thought was not very comforting.

While in bed one night my left leg felt itchy. Normally, I would have reached down and scratched my leg with one of my hands. But that night I instinctively used my right foot to scratch. I nearly jumped out of bed with fright. The sensation of my sprawling toes touching my leg was so unfamiliar that I thought another creature was in bed with me. It was a long time until I could calm myself down.

I kept outgrowing shoes. My right foot had changed shoe sizes, from 10 to 13, and now I was changing shoes again to accommodate an increased width. I had moved from the common D width to the more exotic EE.

And shoes were expensive! I couldn't ask my parents to pay for new shoes without raising a lot of questions. So, I had to pay for them myself.

One day, I thought of a way to save money on shoes. I grabbed my wallet and headed to the sporting goods store by myself.

At the store, I found a EE-width soccer shoe that fit just right. I sat down on a chair with a shoebox in my hand, waiting for a clerk. Finally one arrived, a young guy wearing canvas basketball shoes. I always look at the shoes the clerk is wearing when I'm in a shoe store.

"I like this shoe," I said holding up the right shoe. "I just want to buy this one."

"You only want to buy one shoe?" asked the clerk, just making sure he heard me right.

"Yes, just one," I said.

"It looks to me like you have two feet," said the clerk, raising his eyebrow.

"True."

"So why would you only want one shoe?" asked the clerk.

"I'm a field-goal kicker, and I like having a different feel on my kicking foot," I said.

"Very interesting. I've never had this situation before. I'll go ask the manager," he said, and he walked into the back room.

A couple minutes later, he returned. "We only sell them in pairs. You have to buy both shoes."

"Can I buy one this week and the other one next week?"

"No, you have to buy them both at the same time. You can buy them both this week, or you can buy them both next week. But you can't buy them separately."

Well, it had been worth a try. And really, I could understand where he was coming from. Who would buy the other shoe? What were the chances of a size 13 EE *left-footed* field-goal kicker walking into the store? I shelled out $60 for new soccer shoes and headed out the door.

When I arrived home, I grabbed my football cleat and my new soccer shoes and walked outside. I moved the chair to the edge of the patio so my feet would rest in the grass. I put on the football cleat first. Next I opened the box with the soccer shoes and pulled out the right shoe. I slipped on the shoe and laced it up tight. It looked bigger, but because of the way the football cleat was made, the soccer shoe didn't look *that* much bigger. If anyone noticed the difference in size, I could just say that I needed to wear thicker socks and a bigger shoe on my kicking foot because I was booting it so hard.

I tromped over to the practice net that I had set up in the middle of the yard and kicked a few practice field goals into the net.

And you know what? The shoe felt great.

22.

The next day after practice I stopped by the lab to drop off Ipoo.
Elko was once again sitting with his big feet on the table, writing
in his notebook. He seemed very intent. Suddenly, without
looking up, he grabbed his spray can of knockout gas and pointed
it in my direction.

"Who is it?" he asked, still looking at his notebook.

"It's me, Ivan," I said quickly. "Good grief. Is that how you
greet your guests?"

"Most of the time."

"What if it had been Dr. Carlson?"

"He's out of town with the quarantined patients. And
besides, I can tell it's him from his footsteps. I have very keen
powers of perception."

I didn't want get into a discussion about Elko's powers of
perception, but I was interested in what he was writing. I hoped it
was scientific research on my condition.

"What are you writing?" I asked.

"It's a story."

"Is it about a boy who has a gorilla leg and the guy named Elko who's trying hard to find a cure?" I asked, looking him in the eye. But he remained undeterred.

"No, it's not. It takes place in the Middle Ages. Up in the Alps, there's a village of Cyclopes, giant creatures with one huge eye in the middle of their heads."

"I know what a Cyclops is," I said.

"None of the villagers in the valley below have ever seen the Cyclopes because they rarely go far into the mountains where the Cyclopes live. The Cyclopes eat goats and ibexes, but a disease has struck the mountain herds. Many of the goats and ibexes have died, leaving little food for the Cyclopes."

"Wait a minute, Elko. What's an ibex?"

"They're sort of like goats or sheep, but they have long, ram-like horns." Elko paused for a moment and crunched up his lips in distaste, deep in thought. Sometimes when he made that face he was about to go on a rant about one of his pet peeves. I could tell that it was one of those times.

"You know, I don't know why your high schools and colleges are always using the same old names for your sports teams," he said. "Everywhere you go the names are the same. It's

Cougars, Lions, Bulldogs, whatever. You should juice it up. Cyclopes, Ogres, and Ibexes."

"I can understand calling a team the Ibexes maybe, but most people don't want to be referred to as a Cyclops. The same goes with ogres. I mean, the girls' volleyball team doesn't want to be known as the Ogres."

"What's wrong with ogres," asked Elko, puzzled. "Ogres are very strong."

"Yeah, but they're also mean and ugly and have bad breath and—"

"They don't have bad breath," interrupted Elko.

"Of course an ogre has bad breath. They get it from eating seals and onions and wild pigs."

"Ogres don't eat seals. They live in woodlands and mountains, nowhere near the ocean. Why would you think an ogre eats seals?"

"I don't know. In fact, I don't know much about ogres, except they're mean and ugly and probably have bad breath," I said, exasperated. I hadn't come to talk about ogres.

Elko seemed satisfied that he had made his point and continued. "So the Cyclopes are running short of food, so they hike down from the mountains to where the people live. What do they find? Herds of goats sitting in pens outside the village. The

Cyclopes aren't too civilized, and they don't know anything about breeding animals, so they think that the villagers have stolen the goats from their hunting grounds. The angry Cyclopes attack the village and steal all the goats. Naturally, the villagers are terrified, because a Cyclops is about three times the size of a human, and they carry huge clubs or spears. Even their guard dogs, the St. Bernards, are no match for the Cyclopes."

"Sounds brutal," I said.

"Indeed," said Elko. "From then on, the Cyclopes attack once a year in the fall and steal all the villagers' goats. Finally, one of the villagers returns from Africa with a magic potion he has gotten from a shaman. It contains essence of rhinoceros. The villagers sprinkle it on the St. Bernards. Within a week, they have become 700-pound *rhinards,* a cross between a St. Bernard and a rhinoceros. Are you with me so far?"

"Uh-huh," I said.

"So the villagers prepare for the epic battle between the rhinards and the Cyclopes." He paused.

"Then what happens? Who wins?"

"They both do," said Elko. "And they live together."

"Well, that's a nice peaceful ending to your story, Elko," I said. "The villagers and the Cyclopes find a way to work it out."

"No, the Cyclopes and the rhinards live together," said Elko.

"What about the villagers?"

"They don't do so well."

"What happens?"

"I'm glad you asked," said Elko, positively beaming. "Here's where the story gets good. As the rhinards charge the Cyclopes, something ignites in the primitive part of their brain. The rhinards realize that they share a common history with the Cyclopes. Indeed, before they became extinct in 300 BC, the rhinards had been the loyal pets of Cyclopes. So the rhinards join the Cyclopes, and they attack the villagers together, sacking the village and chasing the villagers off a cliff."

"Elko, that's a horrible story!" I said, appalled.

"It's a surprise ending."

"Yeah, but the poor villagers were attacked by their own rhinards. Is this some sort of horror story?"

"No, it's a kid's story."

"A kid's story? That's not a kid's story. What kind of person would consider that a kid's story?"

"I would. I grew up near the Black Forest reading Grimm's Fairy Tales."

I thought about this, but only for a second. I was about to say something, but Elko spoke first.

"I don't know what it is with you kids these days," he said. "Always wanting a happy ending, wanting things to come together in the end. Sometimes bad things happen."

"Yes, but they don't deserve bad things to happen to them."

"Why not?

"Because they are just kids. No one wants to read about terrible things happening to Hansel and Gretel. It's bad enough that the witch puts them in a cage to fatten them up."

"I thought that the story would be better if the witch ate Hansel. Gretel would have learned a valuable lesson. No more nibbling on people's houses after that!"

"You *are* an ogre, you know that?"

Elko laughed. "Well, that's what happens when kids go sneaking off into the forest." He paused for a moment, his eyes bright with mirth. "Or sneak out of their tent at night and into someone's laboratory." At this Elko roared with laughter, slamming his fist down on the soda can, flattening it into a disk while little drops of cola sprayed through the air.

"Oh, nice," I said, wiping the soda droplets off my sweatshirt. Elko continued to howl with laughter.

"So you think I should be chased off some cliff by a pack of angry rhinards?"

"Of course not, we need you for the football team," said Elko, chuckling.

"What if I wasn't on the football team?"

"But you are."

"What if I wasn't?"

"Who knows," blurted Elko. He was still very amused. He picked up his pen and tapped it on the counter a few times.

"Elko," I said. "Why are we discussing rhinards when you've got your own real-life cross species experiment sitting right in front of you."

Elko crossed his arms, leaned back in his chair, and looked at me. "That's a story that can't be told," he said, finally.

"Is it a story that can be solved? What if I just stopped kicking the ball so well? Would that inspire you to get to work?"

"If you stop kicking the ball, I stop working on the cure," he said, crossing his arms and pouting. He could be a real baby.

"Elko, I just thought I'd tell you about my foot. It's grown from a size 10 D to a size 13 EE. What do you think about that?"

Elko's eyes flashed for a moment and he leaned forward. "I don't like it. It's not affecting your kicking, is it?"

"Well, not yet. But I'm noticing that my big toe is beginning to drift to the left."

"There are only two games left."

"It'll be okay for two games. But that's the limit, Elko. After that, I can't promise that my foot won't be noticeable. In fact, I had to buy new shoes last night. Set me back $60, Elko. You wouldn't want to make a contribution, would you?"

"You're an amateur, kid. Amateurs can't accept gifts," he said.

"Oh puh-leeze! After all the money you made on my games? You owe me! And it's not just the football shoes. I've had to change out all my shoes. Twice!"

"I owe you a cure," he said. "And speaking of that, I spoke with Doc Carlson about an hour ago. He said he's developed an antidote to your gorilla leg condition. It can be administered to you through a series of injections spaced over a couple of weeks. In other words, you are going to return to normal. No more gorilla leg."

"Why didn't you tell me that right away?" I exclaimed. "All this talk about Cyclopes and rhinards. This is big news!"

"All of the test subjects lived."

"What?"

"All the test subject lived. I just thought I'd tell you that."

This statement hit me like a 250-pound defensive lineman. I guess I never considered that any of the test subjects might *die.* I had a flash of anxiety.

"What do you mean by that? You didn't expect anyone to die, did you?"

"No," said Elko. "Not really."

"What do you mean *not really*?"

"No, we didn't expect anyone die," he said. "They didn't wither up, go crazy, or anything like that either. One of the subjects developed a facial tick, where he'd snort and make a strange clicking sound."

"That's terrible!" I shouted, alarmed.

"It's funny, his name is Henry. I had a pet guinea pig named Henry. Of course, my Henry didn't snort and click. Guinea pigs aren't real pigs, you know."

"I don't care about your guinea pig! I care about the guy who's running around snorting and clicking? Did the symptoms go away?"

"Not yet, but I think the virus caused it. I don't think it was caused by the medication we gave him," said Elko flatly. "So you don't need to worry."

"Don't need to worry? Are you sure? I don't want to go around snorting and clicking. Girls don't like guys who run around snorting and clicking. People in the cafeteria line don't like it when someone in front of them is snorting and clinking."

"Don't get all hyper, kid. You won't snort and click. And it was more like a grunting sound anyway."

"I don't want to go around grunting and clicking either. You're not making me feel any better about this," I said.

"I'm telling you, it was probably caused by the virus. And even if it was caused by the antidote, he was just one guy out of twenty," said Elko.

"It would be just my luck."

"C'mon, this is good news. Dr. Carlson has finally found and antidote to your condition. You're going to lose the gorilla leg."

I didn't like the risks of side effects, but we were in uncharted territory, and of course there were some risks. But what were the risks of not taking the antidote? Gorilla-hood, for one. I could turn into a gorilla or something similar, maybe a Sasquatch. I'd have to take the antidote. No delaying it. I made up my mind.

"I'll expect the antidote soon," I said. "I don't think I can carry this off much longer. There's a kid on my team who's been giving me some grief. He's been telling my teammates that there's something fishy about me. Though he's not having much luck. Most of my teammates are thrilled with my new kicking game."

Elko stood up from his chair. "What? Who is this kid? I'll crush him into a ball!"

"He's the halfback."

"Which one?"

"Tommy Dittmore, number 21."

Elko thought for a moment. "Number 21?" he asked.

"Yeah."

"I can't crush him into a ball," said Elko, sitting down in the chair. "He's too good a player. We need him," said Elko.

"You're loyalty to me is astonishing," I said sarcastically. "Anyway, I didn't bring it up so you could crush him into a ball. I brought it up to let you know that suspicions have been aroused."

"Two more games, kid. Then you get the antidote."

"Promise?"

"Promise."

23.

With all that was going on, I was having a bit of difficulty concentrating on my studies. But I realized that I needed to buckle down and hit the books.

One evening I sat down at my desk in the corner of my room. I looked out the window at the kicking equipment in the backyard. Slowly I let my thoughts of football fade into the background. It was time get to work on my German lessons.

Yes, German. My grandparents on my dad's side had emigrated from Czechoslovakia, and German was the closest language to their native tongue. After I got good at it, I thought I could speak with them in German. For that matter, I could also practice with Elko if I wanted to.

But to be honest, I was having a tough time with it. German isn't an easy language to pick up. Spanish might have been a more practical language. But I had chosen German and I was going to stick with it.

We had just started a new book in our class called *Der Vervandlung,* or as it's known in English, *The Metamorphosis,* by Franz Kafka. I cracked open the book and read the first sentence: "Als Gregor Samsa eines morgens aus unruhigen Träumen erwachte, fand er sich in seinem Bett zu einem Ungeziefer verwandelt."

Hmmm, I thought, *that's a whale of a first sentence Very difficult.* I only understood about half of it. I hoped the rest of the book wasn't that hard. I stared at the sentence again. I wasn't sure what it meant, something about a guy named Gregor Samsa who had a troubling dream and woke up as an *Ungeziefer,* whatever that was.

What the heck, I thought, *I could type it into Google translator, but why not call Elko? He'd probably enjoy translating this for me.* I dialed his number.

"Yeah?"

"That's how you answer your phone, Elko?" I asked.

"Yeah," he said. "So what's on your mind?"

"I'm taking German class, and I thought you could translate a sentence for me."

"You never told me you were taking German. I'm very touched. Is it because of me?"

"No, it's because of my grandparents. I started taking German before I even met you."

"Hmm. I was almost flattered."

"Can you translate a sentence for me?"

"Ja, Ich kenne, aber du muss geben mir acht und zwanzig dollars."

"I'm not giving you $28," I said.

"Just testing you."

"Okay, here's the sentence," I said. I picked up my book and recited the first sentence to Elko.

"Oh, that's a good sentence," said Elko, "one of my favorites."

"What does it mean?"

"Allow me to translate: 'As Gregor Samsa awoke one morning from uneasy dreams, he found himself transformed in his bed into a gigantic insect.'"

"Are you making that up?"

"No, that's exactly what it means."

"He was transformed into a gigantic insect?"

"Yep."

I was quiet for a moment, thinking this over. "Well, I guess I don't have it so bad," I said.

"That's right," said Elko.

"Things could be worse. I only have a gorilla leg. I haven't been transformed into a giant insect."

"You've got the right attitude, kid. Plus, you're having a good time kicking field goals," said Elko.

"I feel like I should at least tell Coach about the gorilla leg," I said.

"No way, kid, don't drag Coach into this. The next thing you know you and Coach would be sharing side-by-side jail cells."

"No way."

"Yes, way. This gorilla thing is just one part—a very important part—of a secret mission involving dozens of government agents."

"Are you serious?"

"I shouldn't even be telling you this much. The only reason I'm involved is because Dr. Carlson and I have done some work for this particular secret agency before. And, of course, we are experts in zoology with access to a municipal zoo.

"But the most important thing," Elko continued, "is for you to keep your mouth shut. Otherwise, you'd be jeopardizing the safety of our secret operatives. You don't want to do that."

"Alright, I'll keep it to myself. I guess it won't be too long now before I get the antidote."

"That's right. Try to enjoy yourself. You've got it good. You only had to buy one new shoe. If you were a giant cockroach, you'd need six new shoes."

"I'll try to keep it in perspective," I said.

"Keep practicing all three."

"All three? What do you mean all three?"

Your kicking, punting, and German."

"Oh, for heaven's sake," I said.

"Auf wiedersehen," said Elko.

"Lebe wohl," I said and hung up the phone.

24.

We were playing the Bridgeton Corsairs in the semifinal game. They had a couple of players that seemed familiar to me, huge guys. I could have sworn those players had graduated the year before, but I could have been wrong. Needless to say, they were going to be a tough opponent.

It was a beautiful fall day. Rain had fallen on the field earlier in the week, but it had fully seeped into the ground, giving the sod a soft yet sturdy feeling. I took a big whiff of air through my nose, inhaling the robust smell of the thick, healthy grass. It was time to play football. Our kicking team ran onto the field.

I kicked off. I booted a beauty into the back of the end zone. Now that I'd grown used to my gorilla leg, there was nothing unusual about that. What *was* unusual was that the receiver was ready for the kick. He caught the ball and elected to run it out of the end zone. He had a funny, jagged running style, but he was quick and he dodged two defenders. We finally tackled him at the 25-yard line.

We had arrived. No one was taking us for a fluke anymore. The element of surprise was gone, and now teams were ready for us, with game plans designed to minimize our strengths.

Despite the Corsairs' game plan, our offense was really clicking in the first half, scoring two touchdowns on long drives and gaining enough yardage on two other drives to allow me to kick a pair of field goals. When the first half ended, we were ahead 20–14.

As a team, we were feeling pretty good when we jogged into the locker room at halftime. I felt good, too. It seemed the on-field problem with Tommy was in the past. He had blocked very well each time I had punted. And I was happy about my contribution to the game. I felt like we were going to win this one and move onward to the finals.

But the second half was a different story. I don't know what their coach said to motivate them, or what changes he made to the game plan, but their team came out in the second half with some fierce offensive firepower. They scored a touchdown on their opening drive, then ran it in for two points.

After they kicked off, we went three and out and had to punt. I booted a good one, but their punt return man was the same quick and agile player that handled the kickoffs. He ran it back to the 30-yard line. They ran a sweep, picking up 15 yards. Next, their halfback ran it up the middle, making seven yards. A quick slant to the right and a missed tackle netted them another 12 yards.

I looked into the stands and saw Elko pulling his hair out. By the next play, he had disappeared. I wondered if he'd gotten so frustrated that he simply left the game. But as the Corsair halfback rounded the line of scrimmage for a sweep left, Elko reappeared—not in the stands, but on the sidelines! To say he was acting strangely would be an understatement. His upper body was tilted, at the ready, as if at any moment he would dash onto the field.

He was also holding an aerosol can.

"You crazy man!" I shouted, leaping up from my seat. But there was no way he could hear me. My shout evaporated into the noise of the stadium. Not that it would make a difference anyway. Even if he had heard me, he would have ignored me. I couldn't see his face, but I could just imagine it: his teeth clenched in a sinister smile, his eyes wild and crazy, his finger itchy on the spray top of the can, waiting for the running back.

Just as Elko sidestepped onto the field to blast the advancing running back with his   private blend of knockout gas, the referee blew his whistle, held one hand in the air, and gestured frantically at the sideline.

The Corsair halfback had stepped out of bounds.

I plopped back onto the bench, exhaled, and wiped a bead of sweat from my brow. The ref had been watching the halfback so closely that he had not seen Elko step onto the field. One of the officials on the sidelines had a few words with Elko, after which Elko shrugged and returned to his seat.

The game would go on. I looked at the faces in the crowd behind me. No one was aware of the disaster that had just been adverted. I wondered what the German words were for "loose cannon."

We got a defensive stop. They did not score on that drive. On fourth down and one, Zeph made a remarkable tackle, preventing their fullback from making a first down.

After that, the tables turned. We revved up the offense again, scoring two touchdowns and winning the game 34–22.

25.

Things were going well. The semifinal victory was behind us, and my popularity had crested to a new height. I hadn't paid for a meal at the Haven in five weeks. It seems everyone wanted to pick up the check for Super Booter.

One evening after practice, a group of us rode over to the Haven for a bite to eat. While a bunch of the guys were up milling around, I sat alone with Kipper.

"So, Kipper," I said, stirring the ice in my soda with a straw. "Would you still like me if I didn't kick 50-yard field goals?"

Kipper looked down, took a bite of French fry, and said, "Would you like yourself, if you didn't kick 50-yard field goals?"

Ouch! Where did that come from? I felt like a quarterback who was thrown for a loss of 12 on the play. Time-out on the field! I crammed about six French fries into my mouth to give myself time to think up an answer to that zinger. As I munched away, I really couldn't think of anything to say except for the obvious thing, the honest thing, the first and only thing that popped into my mind.

"One day we'll see," I said. "And I hope it's not too soon."

26.

One day I strolled into the lab and found Elko sitting in his chair with his elbows on the lab table, his big hands under his chin, staring straight ahead, apparently deep in thought.

"Am I disturbing you?"

"Yes, but come in anyway," he grunted.

I waited for him to say something, but he continued to sit there with his head in his hands.

"Should I come back later?"

"No," he said glumly.

"Well, what's going on?"

"Springfield High is canceling its football program after this year," he said, shaking his head.

"That *is* bad news. That's an easy win removed from our schedule," I said.

"Their principal said the cost of running the program was too high," he said. "That's the second article this week I've read about a school canceling its program."

"Is that why you're bummed out?" I asked. "Elko, that's only two schools. It's not a big deal.

"That's only two schools that we've heard of. There's probably hundreds more. What's going to happen to America?"

I looked at Elko to see if he was kidding, but he wasn't. He had a look of sadness and anguish.

"Geez, Elko, it's not the end of the world," I said. "America will go on," I said.

"I hope so," he muttered.

"And there's always baseball."

"How can you be so glib?" he demanded. "This is a disaster. America's spirit is on trial. How can you mention baseball?"

"Actually, baseball is supposed to be America's game," I offered.

"Of course it's not! Maybe before World War II. Before they really started using the forward pass. Maybe before television. But now football is America's sport."

I looked at him and shrugged my shoulders. I didn't have an answer. I was only trying to help. He wasn't having any of it. Two teams canceled their football programs and he was acting like it was a national disaster.

"Baseball might be fun if you were allowed to tackle the runner between first and second base," he said gruffly.

"Tackle people in baseball?

"Yes, tackle," he harrumphed.

"Well, don't get all grumpy."

He was quiet for a moment, staring at the paper on the desk. Finally he spoke. "I mean, I do like baseball, even thought there's no tackling."

"See?" I said. "Baseball's a fun game."

"But, that's a spring sport, he said gruffly. "There will be no America in the fall."

"Well, there's always soccer."

This clearly was the wrong thing to say. He gave me a disgusted look, like he'd just bitten into a rotten apple. "Soccer? I hate soccer. I grew up playing soccer in Europe. Every time I flattened someone the referee would call a foul. It was absurd. I was always getting yellow carded before halftime arrived."

"Well, it *is* against the rules to flatten the other players," I said.

"Exactly! So where's the fun in that? What's a big guy like me to do? You see, that's what I love about America. You guys play sports where it's perfectly okay to smash into each other. In fact, it's a big part of the game. So what are were going to do with all the big people who like to smash into each other?"

I thought for a moment. "How about the Scottish games?"

139

"What are those?"

"It's where big guys pick up logs and throw them as far as they can."

"At other people?"

"No, they just throw them as far as they can."

"Well, what's fun about that?"

"I don't know I was just trying to make you feel better."

"Throwing logs around never made a nation great. In football you use strength, speed and agility. There's teamwork and strategy."

"I agree with you Elko, I love football.

Elko didn't seem to be listening to me. He had his hands under his chin again, sulking.

"My mom doesn't like football so much," I said. "She doesn't like the way we ram into each other like bighorn sheep."

Suddenly, Elko's hands dropped from his chin. He whipped his head around and looked at me with brightened eyes.

"Did Dr. Carlson tell you about the bighorn sheep?"

"No, what are you talking about?"

"Follow me. I've got something to show you." I really didn't have much choice—he grabbed me by the shirt and led me out the door, down the stairs, and out into the zoo. We scooted around a few zoo buildings and came upon a gate. Elko patted his

140

pockets, feeling for his keys.

"I was so excited I forgot my keys," he said.

"Why don't you just ram through it like an offensive tackle?"

I was kidding, of course, but Elko took me seriously. "If I do that, I'll break the gate. I don't want the animals to get out," he said. "We're going to have to climb over."

So we climbed over the fence and walked along a path, through some trees. We came to a clearing where two hoofed animals, white-gray in color, were grazing.

"There they are," said Elko.

"What are those?" I asked.

"They're male bighorn sheep."

"I thought bighorn sheep had horns. Isn't that why they're called bighorns?"

"I was able to get some without horns. It's a genetic mutation. But they still behave like bighorns. I'll show you."

He walked over to a shed and opened the creaky tin door. He pulled out two football helmets. They were modern football helmets, the kind NFL players wear, but they were missing facemasks.

"Check it out, one is for the Rams, which I thought would be appropriate. The other is from the 49ers. The Rams and the 49ers are in the same division." Elko walked over and put a helmet on each of the sheep. It was immediately apparent why there were no facemasks: their long snouts stuck straight out of the helmet.

"Watch," said Elko. He clapped his hands together, making a sharp, loud sound. The rams immediately stopped grazing and ran at each other, smacking their helmets together, making a loud clattering. I looked over at Elko and he was beaming with glee.

"You see? I trained them to do this. I'm studying the structure of football helmets, and these sheep are the perfect test subjects. I record information and tweak the helmets. I'm trying to make a safer one."

A safer football helmet *would* be a welcome invention. Nevertheless, it was an absurd situation. Here were two sheep wearing helmets ramming headlong into each other. Up close, they were very large animals and when they reared up on their hind legs and collided helmet to helmet, it made a frightful sound.

Elko was just standing there watching the sheep butt heads. "I'm also studying the bighorn sheep themselves," he said. "I've been taking some genetic samples."

I looked at him severely. "If you tell me you're going to mix those genes with 1,700 percent growth hormone I'm going to scream."

"It had crossed my mind, but I decided against it."

Elko watched the sheep bash into each other for a little while longer. Then he clapped his hands and blew a whistle and the sheep stopped butting heads, as though it were a real football game and the ref had just blown the whistle.

Elko took their helmets off and walked over to the shed, the sheep trotting cheerfully behind him. He ducked into the shed while the sheep waited outside, then popped back outside with a large platter. The sheep were prancing back and forth excitedly.

"What it that?"

"It's a pie," he said.

"A pie? What kind of pie?"

"It's a pumpkin pie. Bighorn sheep love pumpkin pie."

Elko put the pumpkin pie on the ground and the sheep dove headlong into the pie and began chomping away.

"Good game, you guys," he said to the sheep.

27.

One afternoon my phone rang, a number I didn't recognize. It was Dr. Carlson, calling from a different phone.

"Ivan," he said, "I'm back in town and I'd like to see you."

I wanted to ask, "Do you have the antidote?" But there was something in his tone that didn't sound right.

"What's up? Is something the matter?" I spit out. "Have you discovered the antidote?"

"It's almost finished. I've had some problems with the formula. But it will be ready today."

This is good news, I thought. But suddenly I got a gnawing feeling in my stomach. What would my game, and my life, be like without the gorilla leg? The final game was coming up! I couldn't let the team down. On the other hand, would it be fair to play with a gorilla leg, if I knew there was a cure available? And what would Dr. Carlson say if I said I wanted to delay treatment?

"If I take the antidote today," I asked, "how long will it be before the gorilla leg wears off?"

"Unfortunately, it could take about two weeks," said Dr. Carlson.

I felt a grin spreading across my face. The time frame was perfect. I would lose the gorilla leg, but *after* the big game. Luck was on my side.

"Are you sure about that, Dr. Carlson? I mean, that it will take two weeks?"

"Yes, we've done a number of studies, even before you were injected with the serum. You won't notice much regression of the gorilla attributes until the second week. The second week, however, is marked by rapid change."

"Wow, this is great news!" I blurted excitedly.

"You sound happy," said Dr. Carlson. "I thought you might be a little distressed about the length of time that it would take for your leg normalize. But I guess if I were you, I'd be happy that an end was in sight."

"Oh, yes, I'm happy that all of this is coming to an end," I said. I realized that Dr. Carlson was clueless about how much the upcoming football game meant to me—and Elko, for that matter.

"I might be able to speed up the antidote with a special booster, but I'd rather not inject you with any unnecessary serums."

"Oh, yeah, I wouldn't want that. Let's just take it nice and slow," I said.

"So why don't you come in to the lab tomorrow and I'll give you the first shot. Then we'll give you the next shot on Saturday. Can you make it both days?"

"Tomorrow won't be a problem. But on Saturday it'll have to get there after my football game."

"I will be out of town from Saturday afternoon until the following Wednesday. It's important that we keep the correct spacing between these shots. How about 11 o'clock?"

I thought about it. We had a team chalk talk at ten that morning, which would last about 45 minutes. The stadium was only a five-minute walk from the zoo, and the game wasn't until five o'clock.

"Alright, I'll come in tomorrow at three o'clock, after school, and on Saturday at 11," I said.

"I'll see you then," said Dr. Carlson.

28.

After school on Wednesday, I took the bus downtown to the zoo. When I entered the lab, I saw the familiar faces of Dr. Carlson, Elko, and Ipoo.

"Come in, Ivan," said Dr. Carlson.

Elko gave me a look that said, "Not a word about betting on football games or else. In fact, I was surprised that he hadn't called me to warn me about keeping my mouth shut. Maybe Dr. Carlson hadn't told him that I was coming in that day.

"Let me see that leg," said Dr. Carlson.

"Alright," I said and stripped down to my boxer shorts.

"My word!" shouted Dr. Carlson as he saw my hairy and muscular leg. I hadn't shaved in a couple of days and the hair had grown back. "That's incredible!"

I gave him a puzzled look. "What do you mean?"

"Er, I mean from a scientific standpoint," said Dr. Carlson. "I certainly hope to get your leg back to normal as soon as possible," he quickly added.

"And how long will that take?" asked Elko.

"Two weeks," Dr. Carlson and I said in unison.

Elko nodded at me, satisfied.

Dr. Carlson drew some serum from a vial and walked over to where I was sitting. I still had my pant leg rolled up. He jabbed the needle into my leg and pushed down on the plunger.

Once again, it felt a little bit like a bee sting.

Dr. Carlson looked at my leg. He seemed a little more troubled by what he saw this time.

"The first two or three injections will only keep the gorilla attributes from advancing. After your body adjusts we will start the injections to bring your leg back to normal."

"So, no real changes for at least a couple of weeks."

"Yes, then we start to increase the dosage. I have an extra dose of gorilla serum on hand, just in case your leg shrinks too rapidly. We don't want sagging skin or muscle loss. I've refined serum. It works very quickly."

"Keep that shot handy, just in case."

"I will, if you make sure to keep that leg hidden. We can't afford any revelations at this point."

"Trust me, I'll be careful."

29

The next two days dragged on. I was vigilant about my leg, constantly monitoring it for strength. All the tests I performed showed that I was kicking as well as ever, with no reduction in distance.

I was ready to play.

At last, game day arrived. I woke up at 8:30, well rested. After a good breakfast, I drove my old beater down to the practice field for the team meeting. Coach gave a long speech about teamwork, telling us if we all pulled together like we had throughout the season, we would win this one and bring the glory back to Ellerbach High.

We reviewed the game plan and then gathered up for the cheer.

"One, two, three! Beat the Tigers!"

After the team meeting, I strolled outside and drove to the zoo. I showed the cashier my membership card and headed to the vet hospital.

Once again, Dr. Carlson, Elko, and Ipoo were present in the large room. Elko was pacing back and forth as Dr. Carlson sat in his lab chair reading some charts. Ipoo was grooming himself in the corner.

"Good morning," said Dr. Carlson as I entered the room.

"Hello," I said brightly. "How is everyone?"

Elko grunted.

"Elko wants me to wait to give you the next shot until after the football game," said Dr. Carlson.

"What would it hurt?" said Elko. "The kid's got a big game this afternoon. What if there was a reaction to the shot? He might have to sit out."

"Elko, he's already had the first shot. There was no reaction. He'll be fine," said Dr. Carlson.

"You're putting it right in his kicking leg," said Elko.

"That's because it's the gorilla leg. We're not going to inject him in the normal leg," said Dr. Carlson, with some exasperation.

"I don't like it," said Elko.

Why are you so invested in this?" said Dr. Carlson. "It doesn't seem to bother Ivan." While Dr. Carlson spoke, he prepared the syringe full of gorilla antidote. Elko was making me nervous. Did he know something that I didn't? I wasn't sure. But I was sure that I didn't want to have a gorilla leg for life.

I bared my leg. Dr. Carlson was just about to jab me when Elko spoke.

"What about sudden muscle shrinkage?"

"Elko, we've done the research. We really don't expect any shrinkage at all until the second week. Plus, we have that original gorilla serum to reverse any hyper-shrinkage."

Elko seemed to accept this answer. "Okay," he said.

"Good," said Dr. Carlson. "Now please don't interrupt me this time."

Dr. Carlson gave me the injection, and just as he did an outrageously loud clattering rang out from the utility closet at the far end of the room. Elko jumped to his feet, dashed across the room, and swung open the closet door.

Inside the closet stood Tommy Dittmore, tape recorder in hand, eyes wide open with surprise as he saw Elko on the other side of the door. Although he was accustomed to dodging large defensive linemen, Tommy clearly wasn't expecting someone the size of Elko to be standing between him and the doorway. He tried a few halfback moves. He faked to the left, then back to the right, trying to slip under Elko's arm. Elko bumped him with his hip and shoved him into the large room.

Tommy stood in the middle of the room for an instant, then made a dash for the hallway door. But before he could take two full steps, Elko seized him by the shirt, and quickly raised his other hand. *Psssssst* came the sound of the aerosol spray. Elko gave Tommy a little shove as he released him.

Tommy ran forward about six steps, each one slower than the one before. He made it as far as the swinging doors of the laboratory, then leaned against the doors and collapsed, falling through the doors halfway into the hallway. His tape recorder smashed against the ground.

We all gathered around him, as he lay crumpled on the floor.

"That'll teach the little puke," Elko said. "That was the stronger gas."

He grabbed Tommy by the feet and dragged him back into the room, then picked up the broken pieces of the tape recorder and tossed them in the trash can.

"He looks like a teenager," said Dr. Carlson. "What would a teenager be doing in the closet?"

"He's on my football team," I said.

"I still don't understand," said Dr. Carlson. "Why would he be spying on us?"

"I think he wanted to find out how I could be kicking the ball so far. He was jealous," I said.

"He should have been at home studying his playbook," grumbled Elko. "Which position is he anyway?"

"He's one of the halfbacks," I said.

"What?" said Elko, concerned. "Which halfback?"

"Tommy Dittmore. You wouldn't recognize him. You've never seen him with his helmet off."

"He's not number 21, is he?"

"Yes," I said. "Number 21 is Tommy Dittmore."

"What!" shouted Elko. "We need him in the big game! Why didn't you stop me?"

"I didn't have time to," I shouted back. "You've got a quick trigger finger!"

Elko dashed over to Tommy and knelt down by his head. "Wake up kid," he said, slapping Tommy's face. But Tommy had no reaction.

Truth be told, I had mixed feelings about Tommy getting blasted in the face with knockout gas. He deserved whatever headache he would have when he woke up. But I thought about Coach's talk about teamwork. Tommy was part of the Bulldog team. And quite frankly, I realized that we weren't going to have much of a chance of winning the game without him.

"We've got to revive him," I said very quietly my heart not completely in it.

"What?" shouted Elko.

"I said we've got to revive him," I uttered with a little more spirit.

"Of course we do!" shouted Elko. He lifted up Tommy's eyelids, but they just snapped shut when he let go. He poked him in the ribs. No reaction. Elko looked flummoxed.

"Geez, Elko, why'd you have to spray him?" I said. "Couldn't you just have grabbed him by the shirt and thrown him against the wall like a normal thug?"

Elko jutted out his chin and stared at the wall for a moment. He seemed to be considering my question.

"The spray is more fun," said Elko flatly.

At least it was an honest answer.

"He invented it, you know," said Dr. Carlson brightly.

At that moment, I'm sure Elko wished he hadn't invented his knockout gas. But the genie was already out of the aerosol can, so to speak.

"Put the coffee on, Ivan," said Elko as he walked over to the deep freeze and pulled out an ice cube tray from among the frozen specimens. He twisted the tray and a dozen ice cubes tumbled into a big metal bowl. He filled the bowl with water and stirred it.

"Why don't you just let him sleep it off?" said Dr. Carlson.

"He's one of our best players, and we have a championship game in a couple hours," I said.

"Why are you so upset about it, Elko?" asked Dr. Carlson. "You're not betting on these games again, are you?" he asked.

"Of course not," said Elko, looking over at Dr. Carlson guiltily. "Alright, maybe a little. Certainly not a lot. Like I said, I'm a fan."

I couldn't tell if Dr. Carlson believed Elko or not. He just stroked his chin a few more times and nodded his head.

Meanwhile, Elko walked over to Tommy and dumped the entire contents of the metal bowl on Tommy's head. The water cascaded over his face and a few ice cubes bounced off his forehead. Tommy responded with a small sputtering cough and then went back to sleep.

"Great!" said Elko, throwing his hands in the air. "Now the team is doomed."

"Let me handle this," said Dr. Carlson, shaking his head at our efforts. He sauntered over to a glass door cabinet, opened it, and pulled out a small cylindrical object. He strolled over to Tommy and knelt down beside him, then broke the cylindrical object in half and stuck it under Tommy's nose.

"Wha-hah!" Tommy coughed and gasped and sat up straight, his eyes like saucers. "Where the heck am I?"

"You're in a veterinary hospital in the zoo," I said.

"How are you feeling, kid?" said Elko.

"I'm not sure," said Tommy. "How did I get here?"

"You were trespassing. If you weren't the star running back we'd have thrown you in the dumpster," said Elko.

Tommy looked at Elko. One second his eyes were like pinwheels, the next they started to close as if he was nodding off again. Slowly, in fits and starts, he regained his consciousness. He coughed some more.

"Is that coffee ready?" shouted Elko.

I poured the coffee into the biggest mug I could find and handed it to Elko.

"Drink this, kid," he said as he handed the cup to Tommy.

"Hot," he said.

Elko grabbed two ice cubes off the floor, quickly rubbed them on his shirt, and plopped them in Tommy's coffee cup. He pulled a pen out of his shirt pocket and stirred the ice.

"Now drink it," he said. "We're running short of time."

Tommy took a tentative sip.

"What's wrong? Is it still too hot?" asked Elko.

"I don't really like coffee," murmured Tommy.

"Yes, you do. Now drink it," commanded Elko.

Tommy did his best and drank it down. When he was finished, he put his cup down on the floor.

"Can you stand up?"

With a little effort, Tommy rose to his feet.

"Would you look at that? Good boy," said Elko, like Tommy was a baby who had taken his first steps.

"Try a few jumping jacks."

Tommy did a few jumping jacks.

Dr. Carlson rolled his eyes, helping himself to a cup of coffee. "What is going on here? This isn't a gymnasium," he said.

Elko ignored Dr. Carlson. He was intently focused on getting the star running back in shape for the game.

"Hmmm. I think we better get him home," said Elko. "His parents are probably wondering about him."

"Not so fast," said Dr. Carlson. "Don't forget about the classified nature of this laboratory."

"C'mon, the kid doesn't remember a thing," said Elko.

"We need to be sure," said Dr. Carlson.

Elko turned to Tommy. "So, kid, why were you hiding in the broom closet?"

"Broom closet?" said Tommy, still a little dazed.

"See?" said Elko to Dr. Carlson.

"Alright, let him go," said Dr. Carlson. "But he should know that he's to speak to no one about his little adventure here. Otherwise, we'll press charges of breaking and entering."

Dr. Carlson walked over to me and whispered, "When you give him a ride home, please inform him that the work we perform in this hospital is top secret. But by no means should you divulge any of the secret information that I have told you."

"What if he asks what we're doing here? I've got to tell him something. Otherwise he'll be suspicious."

"Just let him know it's top secret and that he should keep his mouth shut. Tell him the knockout gas was for first-time offenders. The penalty is much more severe for second-time offenders."

"Okay," I said uncertainly. I walked over to Tommy. "Ready to go?"

Tommy looked at me blankly.

"Yes," he said. He looked incredibly humbled by the whole adventure.

I didn't really want to give Tommy a ride home. But what was I going to do? Leave him there right before the big game?

"I'll give you a ride," I said.

As we were walking out the door, Elko stopped me. Tommy kept walking through the swinging doors.

158

"How's your leg?" asked Elko.

In all the confusion, I had forgotten about the reason I had come to the lab in the first place. Despite Tommy's interruption, I had gotten a full dose of the antidote. Whether it was from all the excitement or the injection itself, my leg felt a little rubbery. But I didn't want to freak Elko out.

"It feels fine," I said.

"Good," said Elko, as he patted me on the back and ushered me out the door.

30.

I walked in silence with Tommy through the hallways of the vet hospital. When we reached the sidewalk leading out of the zoo, I told him, "I know it doesn't look like it, but those guys are involved in some top secret research. The doctor wanted me to tell you that you should keep this whole experience to yourself. Don't mention to anyone what you saw or heard."

"I have no idea what they are doing in there. All I can remember is that someone was talking about gorillas."

I sensed an opening to confuse him.

"Gorillas? What's top secret about gorillas?" I asked.

"How should I know? I just remember getting sprayed in the face with some sort of gas by that Elk guy."

"Elko."

"Whatever."

He really did look bewildered. Elko's knockout gas seemed to have done a number on him.

"Do you remember anything before that?"

"Not really. It's all foggy to me."

"Well, please don't mention anything about the lab to anyone."

"I'd just like to forget the whole thing," said Tommy.

"Good."

We walked over and got into my car. I resisted the urge to ask him why he was hiding in the closet. He still looked a little out of it.

"So, will you be ready for the big game?" I asked.

"Yep," he said. He didn't say another thing until I dropped him off at home. He just stared straight ahead at the road in front of him. As I pulled the car into the driveway he turned to me, and I thought he might be about to explain his actions. Instead, he turned away, opened the door, and hopped out.

"Thanks for the ride," he said.

31.

At home, I checked my email and ate a small meal before going outside to practice kicking into a net. I thought about our opponent, the Tigers. There was no question as to why the Tigers were in the championship game. They had started the season strong and only got better as the season progressed. It would be hard to find a weakness in their team.

I stood before my kicking net, my leg still feeling a little rubbery. It could have been my imagination, but it just didn't feel quite as strong. There was no way to judge the distance of my kicks, since I was booting it into the net. I really didn't have the time to run down to the park where there was a goalpost, so I called Dr. Carlson to ask him about it.

"Hello, Dr. Carlson. It's Ivan," I said.

"Ah, Ivan." Dr. Carlson sounded like he was glad to hear from me. "Did you get that kid home alright?"

"Yes, no problems there. It's just...well...my leg felt a little different while I was kicking in the backyard and I was wondering: is there any chance the shot would be taking effect sooner rather than later?"

I braced myself for his answer. I was really hoping he'd tell me that I was imagining things, that it was all in my head.

"It could be. After I examined your leg I was concerned, so I doubled the dosage," he said.

"What! I have the championship game today!" I shouted.

"Okay, calm down," said Dr. Carlson. "I'm a doctor, not a gambler. Do you want to have a gorilla leg all your life? You are very close to the point of no return. I really had no choice."

I didn't know what to say. I was in full panic mode. I wanted to get into my car and drive to another city. I wanted to go back to my simple life, when I went to school and punted the ball 30 yards.

Sensing my angst, Dr. Carlson offered up some consolation. "Listen," he said. "I doubt the serum can work that fast. You should still be able to kick the ball just as far as before."

"Are you sure? You sound like you're guessing."

"Well, we are in uncharted territory, aren't we?" said Dr. Carlson.

"I guess you're right," I said. But I wasn't consoled. I was scared of letting the team down and thinking of an alias for myself for when I ran away from home and went into hiding.

"I feel that I'm responsible for all this," said Dr. Carlson. "If I didn't get a large amount of serum into you this morning, there was a chance that you might have a gorilla leg for life. Sort of puts one football game into perspective, doesn't it?"

Yes, it did put things into perspective, I thought to myself, *if you were calm and thinking logically.* But I had the biggest football game of my life coming up and the team, the crowd, *everyone,* it seemed, was depending on me.

"What about the original gorilla serum?" I asked. "We could use that to reverse what's happening to my leg."

"I don't recommend it, not now," said Dr. Carlson. "The serum should be used only in case that your leg shrinks too rapidly. You see, we don't want your leg to gain or lose muscle tissue too quickly. If your leg shrinks too rapidly, it might result in sagging skin, stretch marks, that sort of thing."

At this point, I just let it all hang out.

"Dr. Carlson, I'm not worried about sagging skin. I'm worried about having my whole football career crumble, letting down the team."

"I see," said Dr. Carlson. "Well, I will only use the serum if your leg seems to be shrinking dramatically. We want it to shrink, but not too quickly. I'll bring it along to the game. Elko and I are going to the game, you know."

"I thought you were going out of town?"

"Not now. I'm too worried about your leg. I plan to watch it closely. I don't want it to remain a gorilla leg, but I also don't want it to shrink too rapidly."

"Okay," I said, only slightly relieved.

"Stop worrying. You'll be fine. Like I said, you still have most of your gorilla strength. Remember that! Now, go out there and win one for the Gripper."

"The *Gipper*," I corrected.

"Yes, whoever he is," said Dr. Carlson.

32.

I arrived at the stadium at about the same time as everyone else. The players were doing some drills on the field, so I practiced kicking into a net. But I still wasn't getting a good indication of my kicking power.

Zeph ran up to me. He smiled. "You ready, Super Booter?"

"Of course," I lied.

The team warmed up on our side of the field, the quarterback passing to the receivers, the linemen doing half-speed blocking drills, and everyone generally loosening up. Meanwhile, the fans were streaming into the bleachers, wearing the colors of their teams. I could see Ipoo, our mascot, standing on the sidelines in front on the cheering section. High in the bleachers, in the end zone behind the goal posts, was a fan-made target that said "Super Booter Bulls Eye."

I was feeling the pressure. I looked down the field and saw Tommy talking with Coach. He gazed my way, seemed to make eye contact, but looked away after a second or two. I went back to kicking into the net. The rubbery feeling in my leg had gone away, but it still didn't feel as strong as before.

Coach called us together.

"If everyone does his job, we win this one. We've taken it one game at a time all season. Now there's just one game left. You're the best team that ever walked the halls of Ellerbach High. Now let's get out there and prove it to everyone!" shouted Coach. Cheers echoed through the locker room.

"Let's huddle up," shouted Coach.

"One, two, three! Beat the Tigers!" we shouted, and ran out onto the field while applause and cheers erupted from the stands.

The Tigers won the coin flip and elected to receive the football. I trotted onto the field for the opening kickoff. The cheers were already starting.

"Super Booter, Super Booter, ooh, aah! Super Booter, Super Booter, ooh, aah!" shouted the crowd, louder than ever before. I lined up at the 35-yard line and raised my hand. As I lowered my hand, the entire team ran toward the 40-yard line as I kicked the ball. The crowd cheered loudly.

It felt like a good kick. I connected with the bottom third of the ball and felt good, solid contact with the ball. In fact, I kicked it so hard that I had a hard time maintaining my balance after the kick, taking several loping, swirling steps as I tried to steady myself for a run down the field towards the Tigers.

The ball sailed to the Tiger's five-yard line. Certainly not one of the better Super Booter kicks, but nothing to be ashamed of. And the kick had arched high in the air, giving the Bulldog players plenty of time to cover the field. The receiver ran the ball back to the 20-yard line.

I jogged off the field.

"Good kick," said Coach, slapping me on the shoulder.

I relaxed for about five minutes. My leg had felt pretty good during the kick, but now the rubbery feeling was back. I wondered if my leg was "humanizing" during each rubbery episode. Or was it just nervousness? It was impossible to tell. I couldn't research it on the Internet during the game, and even if I could, what would I type in the search engine? "Boy with gorilla leg"?

With six running plays and two short passing plays, the Tigers had moved the ball out to our 46-yard line. At this point, our defense stiffened and the Tigers were forced to punt.

Tommy was back to receive the punt. He caught the ball at the 27-yard line. He tried a few clumsy moves and was creamed at the 28-yard line. Not good. I wondered if he was still drowsy from his experience earlier that day.

Somehow, we got a first down. Then we ran a couple of lackluster running plays, including two handoffs to Tommy. Soon it was fourth down.

I stood back to punt.

"Thirty-seven, 61, hut, hut, HUT!" Reggie hiked the ball directly into my hands. Beautiful.

One step, two steps, BOOM! I put all my might into the punt. The ball sailed upward and downfield. About 40 yards. Not typical Super Booter, but all things considered, not bad. I was feeling a lot better.

We scored first. Tommy didn't seem to be moving the ball very well, so our quarterback handed the ball to Andy Castro on a couple of plays. He ran it down to the six-yard line, but we couldn't punch it into the end zone.

Luckily, a 23-yard field goal was well within my range. I trotted onto the field and kicked it through the uprights. I heard the cheers for Super Booter as I ran off the field and felt a huge relief. If we could keep the field goals at close range, everything would be all right.

The Tigers went three and out, punting the ball to Tommy, who tried a couple of different moves but got creamed again. After a mixture of running and short passing plays, Mullen threw a beautiful pass to Derek Wilcox, our wide receiver, who ran it down to the nine-yard line before being tackled. Mullen handed off to Tommy on the first two plays but he gained a meager three yards. On third down, Mullen threw an incomplete pass.

Looks like it's time to kick, I thought.

I could hear the Super Booter cheers as I jogged onto the field. This would be a 26-yard field goal—again, within my old range. The transitions from center to quarterback to kicker went like clockwork, and I booted it between the goalposts. The score was 6–0, Bulldogs in the lead. I was feeling good.

But the Tigers weren't going away. They got into an offensive rhythm, mixing up their plays and moving the ball quickly down the field. On a quarterback option play, they ran it into the end zone. Touchdown, Tigers. They kicked the extra points and it was 7–6, Tigers in the lead.

We got the ball back and through a series of plays utilizing Tommy, Andy Castro, and Derek Wilcox, we moved the ball to the Tigers' 30-yard line. Coach called me over.

"Kick it through those uprights," said Coach, as he slapped me on the back and pushed me onto the field.

I lined up behind center. This was the moment I had been dreading. It would be a long field goal for anyone in high school, a good 47 yards, but it was within my gorilla-leg range. I could hear the Super Booter cheers as I paced off the steps from where the quarterback would hold the ball.

"Hut, hut, HUT!" The ball was snapped perfectly to Mullen, who spun the ball so the laces faced away. I kicked it as hard as I could. I watched the ball spin end over end through the air and land in the end zone, five yards short of the goal posts.

"Awww," the crowd moaned as I trotted off the field.

"Good try," said Coach, patting me on the back. "Next one will be through, I can feel it. I hope you had your two bowls of oatmeal today."

"Thanks, Coach," I said as I jogged over to the end of the bench, gritting my teeth.

I was relieved to see our team moving the ball again. Whenever we passed the opponent's 15-yard line, I knew I was into my old field goal range again. My leg was feeling hotter than the rest of my body. I wasn't sure what it meant, but strange feelings were not welcome feelings. I wanted the old gorilla leg feeling back.

On a broken play, our quarterback lobbed the ball to our other wide receiver, Raymond "Mondo" McGuiness. He made a few magnificent moves and sprinted 40 yards for a touchdown. The Bulldog crowd roared its approval. I was ecstatic. If we could start scoring touchdowns, it would make my job a whole lot easier. I booted the extra point and it was 13–7 Bulldogs.

But after my kickoff, the Tigers answered the challenge. Through a mixture of running plays and short passes they took the ball down to the five-yard line. On the next play, a quarterback draw play, they scored a touchdown. After the extra point, they led by one point.

With three minutes left in the first half, Coach called me out to try another field goal. The ball was at the 25-yard line, making it a 42-yard kick.

Once again, I could hear the Super Booter cheers from the crowd. I lined up behind the quarterback, who was already kneeling on one knee. I called the signals and Reggie snapped it to the quarterback, who spun the ball in place. Once again I booted it as hard as I could.

I watched the ball sail through the air toward the goalposts. The accuracy was spot-on, but I wasn't sure about the distance. It was going to be close. I watched in dismay as the ball struck the crossbar of the goalpost and bounced forward onto the playing field.

The referee leaned forward and crossed his arms over and over.

"No good," he said.

"That's okay," said Coach as I ran to the sidelines. "There's a lot of football left to be played. Just keep yourself loose."

I trudged over and sat on the end of the bench, looking into the stands. It seemed like the entire school was attending the game. Then I saw Elko gesturing wildly at me.

I held my hands out. "What?" I said.

He couldn't hear me, but I knew he understood me. Nevertheless, he kept gesturing, and started walking down the steps of the stands toward the field. Great, I thought. How would I find time to speak with Elko in the middle of the championship game?

The Tigers weren't going into the locker room at halftime without a fight. Indeed, they put the ball in the end zone again and kicked the extra point.

The half ended with the Tigers ahead 21–13. We trotted off the field into the locker room. Besides Mondo's run after his catch, our playing had been rather lackluster, certainly not championship caliber. Yet Coach was still very much upbeat. He gathered us around for a halftime pep talk.

"Was this our best half of football?" said Coach. "No. Was this our worst? No! We hung in there against the toughest team in the league and we are only eight points down. I'd rather be us than them. You know why, Bulldogs? I'll tell you: Because they have been out there giving their best, trying to defeat us. They have played their best Tiger football and they are only eight points ahead of us. Eight points! We haven't shown them our best. If we go out there and show them true Bulldog football, we will win this thing."

Coach paused and looked us all in the eyes, his voice slowly rising to a crescendo. "If you play like the Bulldogs that I've known all season, I know that we'll grab that championship trophy and take it home to Ellerbach High! Now, let's go out there and win this one for the Gipper!"

We roared and cheered. It seemed like everyone wanted to win one for the Gipper lately. I think only half of us new who the Gipper was, but still, the sentiment struck home and we felt inspired.

"Let's all huddle up," shouted Coach.

"One, two, three! Beat the Tigers!" we shouted. Then we wandered around the locker room, pulling up our socks, re-tying our shoes, and generally getting ready for the second half.

I caught a glimpse of Tommy sitting on the end of the bench, looking sad, almost despondent. I felt a sinking feeling in my stomach. This was not good. We were down by eight at the end of the half, and now our star player was looking like his pet rabbit just died. Again, I wondered if it was Elko's knockout spray that had caused lethargy in our star running back or if it was something else.

As I walked past Tommy, he grabbed the edge of my jersey.

"Ivan," he said. "Can I talk to you over there?" He gestured toward the filthy showers.

"Now?"

"Yes, now. It will only take a second," Tommy said. "Please?"

I was so surprised to hear the word "please" to come out of Tommy, I reluctantly agreed. But not without a fair amount of dread. This certainly wasn't the time to hash out our differences.

When we reached the showers, I braced myself. Tommy looked me in the eye.

"I just wanted to say that I'm sorry," he said.

Whoa! I didn't expect that. Dumbfounded, I looked back at him. He seemed sincere.

"I've been acting like a selfish jerk. I don't know what got into me. But I want to apologize. Maybe it took that big Elk guy spraying me in the face to bring me around," he said.

"His name is Elko," I said.

"Doesn't matter. I just feel bad about spying on you and bad-mouthing you. We're supposed to be playing as a team." Tommy stared at the floor for a moment. "I just wanted to get this off my chest."

"Why you didn't say something earlier, like in the car?" I said.

"I was too ashamed. I was afraid that you'd tell me what you really thought of me. You would have had every right to. But I couldn't have taken it then. Even now I don't feel like myself."

"Would it help if I accepted your apology?"

Tommy brightened. "It would help a lot."

"Then I accept your apology," I said, smiling.

"No hard feelings?"

"Nope. I'm glad you cleared it up."

"Thank you. I feel like a giant weight has been lifted from my shoulders."

"Good. Now can you do me a favor?"

"Anything. You name it."

"Get out there and play your heart out. Let's win this one."

"Right on, Ivan." He gave me a quick hug. "Thanks, bro, I really appreciate it. If there's anything else I can do, just let me know."

"Just get out there and play your hardest. Score some touchdowns and take the pressure off me," I said.

"You got it," said Tommy as he jogged out of the locker room. Quite frankly, I'd never seen him that happy. Maybe Elko's knockout gas could bring peace to the Middle East.

33.

As I was walking back toward the center of the locker room, I saw the door to the parking lot open a crack. In the crack I saw the Elko's unmistakable face peering through. His eyes lit up when he saw me. He began to gesture frantically.

I had just solved the problem with Tommy, and now Elko wanted to talk to me. Somehow I didn't think it involved an apology. I walked past, shaking my head at him. Now was not the time, especially with all the other players and Coach around.

Coach was rallying the team for the second half. "Let's go Bulldogs!" he shouted. The entire team charged out of the locker room and onto the field. I ran with them, then made a quick U-turn and darted back into the locker room.

"You can come out now," I shouted. Elko stepped out from behind the last row of lockers. To my surprise, Dr. Carlson was with him.

"We came to check on how you were doing," said Dr. Carlson. "This is a critical time in the transformation of your leg and—"

"I came along, too," interrupted Elko, "to help in any way I can."

"I don't have time for a doctor's appointment right now," I said to Dr. Carlson. "Besides, I'm wearing full pads." I gestured down at my leg.

But Dr. Carlson ignored my statement and walked over to me. "I can tell by just looking at your calf," he said as he pulled down my sock. He pushed at my calf in several places. "Well, it doesn't seem as though your muscles are shrinking too fast and there's no sagging skin, so it's up to you whether you get the booster shot. I wouldn't recommend it."

"But to be sure," said Elko, "you could get this injection and be certain that you aren't losing muscle to fast." Elko glared at me and nodded his head. "This will ensure that there will be no sagging skin or stretch marks. Having sagging skin on your leg is not a good way to go through life. Girls don't like guys with stretch marks on their legs."

Of course Elko wanted me to take the injection. He'd cash in *big time* if the Bulldogs won the championship. A made or missed field goal could make the difference in the game. So he didn't want to take any chances. Dr. Carlson, on the other hand, didn't seem to care.

I sat for a moment and thought it over. It was tempting to be Super Booter for one more day. I could lead the team to victory. But I had a choice this time, and that hadn't been the case before. Would it be fair to take an injection just to win the game?

I imagined a tiny angel on one of my shoulders and a tiny devil on the other, as if in a scene from a movie.

"Go with the gorilla leg," said the devil.

"Don't do it," said the angel.

I'd like to say that I made the right decision, that I came down on the side of fair play. But I didn't. In fact, I didn't make any decision. I didn't have time to.

Elko wasn't waiting around for me to decide. He was sitting beside me on the bench, and when I looked over I saw that he had the syringe out and was ready to jab me straight through the football pants. Suddenly the door of the locker room burst open, banging against the metal trashcan.

"Where's Super Booter?" shouted a voice.

Surprised, I jumped up, my arms flying outward in alarm, hitting Elko's arm just as it was coming down with the syringe. His hand veered to the side and he jabbed his own leg, injecting the gorilla booster into his thigh.

"I'll be right out," I yelled in a panic to whoever had stuck his head in the locker room looking for me.

"Oh, no!" Elko shouted as he yanked the syringe out of his leg and threw it against the wall. "I wasted our only shot!"

"What happened?" said Dr. Carlson.

"The kid bumped my arm when I was giving him the shot," groaned Elko. "I injected myself with the serum, not him." He stood up, spread his arms out, and shook them in exasperation. "This is a disaster!"

"You'll be alright, Elko," said Dr. Carlson. "We've tested it. It's safe."

Elko looked at Dr. Carlson in amazement.

"*Me?*" he shouted. "I'm not worried about *me*! I'm worried about *him*! His leg is turning back to normal. His last kick didn't even clear the crossbar. Two days ago, he would have drilled it into the stands. And number 21 isn't playing worth a hoot since I sprayed him with knockout gas! We'll never win!"

Elko plopped down on the bench, put his fingers to his temples, and seemed to drift off into deep thought.

At that point it seemed clear that Elko had wagered more than a small amount on the game, but I guess Dr. Carlson was saving his lecture for another time.

Elko, however, wasn't worried about Dr. Carlson. He was

looking for new solutions to his problems.

"I've got it!" he shouted, standing up. "Give me your jersey, Ivan."

"What?"

"I'll go kick. I'm the one with the gorilla leg now." Elko was grabbing my jersey, trying to pull it over my head.

"Are you crazy? You can't go out there. Everyone will wonder how I gained a hundred pounds during halftime. They'll know it's not me. We'll be disqualified."

Elko wasn't listening. He was intent on being the kicker.

"How hard can it be?" he said.

"It's a lot harder than it looks. It's got to go in a straight line," I said.

"Elko, get a hold of yourself!" shouted Dr. Carlson. "No one is going to believe for an instant that you're Ivan. You won't even fit into his jersey. We've got to let things unfold naturally. There's nothing we can do about it now. There are lots of good players on the team. The Bulldogs can still win."

Elko let go of my jersey and sat down on the bench with his head in his hands. He appeared to be accepting that the idea of him showing up as the field-goal kicker was preposterous.

"I'm ruined," he said.

"C'mon, Elko. Give the Bulldogs a chance," said Dr.

Carlson. "They'll win it for the Gripper."

"The *Gipper*," corrected Elko. "Why should I listen to you? You don't even know who the Gipper was."

BANG! The door opened into the trash can again. "Where's Super Booter?" someone shouted.

"Coming!" I said. "Just lacing up my shoe." I turned to Elko and Dr. Carlson. "I gotta go."

"Maybe if I run back to the lab, I can get another dose," said Elko, hopefully.

"There's none left," said Dr. Carlson. "I used it in some experiments earlier this week."

"I gotta go!" I shouted again, more urgently.

Elko stood up, put both hands on my shoulders, and looked me in the eye. "Do your best, kid," he said.

I ran outside and onto the field.

34.

To begin the second half, the Tigers kicked off. Tommy fielded the ball, ran to the left, dodging two tacklers, then back to the center. Eventually, he was brought down at the 50-yard line. A great run-back.

We sustained a long drive but were once again stopped inside the ten-yard line. Coach called me in to kick another close-range kick. The ball was snapped perfectly to the quarterback, who planted the ball and spun the laces to the side. I booted it. I listened. Then I heard the cheers. I exhaled. The kick was good. Score: 21–16, Tigers in the lead.

I kicked to the Tigers, but they couldn't move the ball, so they punted to us. Things were looking pretty good, but three plays later, our quarterback tossed it to the flanker, who was hit immediately. The ball popped out and the Tigers recovered. The opposing stands erupted in cheers.

Our defense ran onto the field, ready to take a stand. However, the Tigers executed their next set of plays very well.

Before we knew it, the ball was on the nine-yard line. First and goal for the Tigers.

On the next play, their quarterback dropped back for a pass. He threw it into the end zone. Zeph put his hands up and tipped the ball. A group of four players dove for the ball. Unfortunately, a Tiger player caught it before the ball hit the ground. Touchdown. After the extra point, the Tigers were up 28–16.

The Tigers kicked off, sending a long, low kick that landed at the ten and bounced into Tommy Dittmore's hands as he was running forward. With a group of four Bulldogs in front of him, he ran up the sideline. The first wave of would-be tacklers were blocked by Bulldogs. As another group of Tigers approached, Tommy dodged them by making a quick cut toward the middle of the field. He cut past few more players and finally was brought down by a leaping tackle at the Tigers' ten-yard line. It was a brilliant and inspired run-back. Tommy was back in full force.

Two plays later, Mullen faked a handoff to Tommy and ran it in for a touchdown. After the extra point, it was 28–23, Tigers in the lead, but with the Bulldogs quickly closing the gap.

We kicked off to the Tigers. They were moving the ball well. But on a blitz, Zeph caught their quarterback seven yards behind the line of scrimmage on a failed option play. The Bulldog crowd cheered wildly. The Tigers couldn't make up the lost yardage and needed to punt.

We were really feeling the momentum now. But we were dealt a nasty blow a few plays later when Reggie Mapu pulled a hamstring and had to limp off the field. This was a disaster for me. Reggie was the most reliable center to ever play the game for Ellerbach High. Now, I would have to adjust to another center — Danny Mapu, Reggie's younger brother, a freshman. I wondered if he had ever snapped the ball in an actual game.

Two plays later we were forced to punt, and I was taking a snap from Danny.

"Gray, 98, hut, hut, hut, HUT!" I shouted while stomping my foot. Danny snapped the ball. It landed perfectly in my hands. Whew!

One step, two steps, BOOT! I kicked that ball, once again, with all my might, trying to compensate for my weakening leg.

But I botched the punt. In trying to kick it so hard, I lost control. The ball sailed out of bounds, 20 yards from the line of scrimmage. I trotted off the field with my head down, but I couldn't help sneaking a look at Elko, who was watching the game with his hand near his mouth, probably chewing his fingernails down to the nubs.

In the next set of downs, the Tigers powered down to the one-

186

yard line on a series of running plays. On a quarterback sneak, they scored. After the extra point, they were ahead 35–23.

We got the ball back. After running for a first down, Mullen called a pass play, throwing it to Mondo McGuiness in the left flat. The pass was high, but Mondo made a leaping catch. The defender couldn't keep up and fell down. Touchdown Bulldogs!

I kicked the extra point. Now the score was 35–30, with the Tigers in the lead as we entered the fourth quarter.

The Tigers tried a screen pass and two running plays, but weren't able get a first down. They punted. The Tigers side of the stadium moaned in frustration, while the Bulldogs side was anxious in anticipation.

Our dreams of a comeback came true ten plays later, with Andy Castro making a key block, allowing Tommy to sprint into the end zone. In the stands the Bulldog fans went crazy!

With the score 36–35 in our favor, we tried for a two-point conversion, but Mullen was stuffed near the line of scrimmage on a quarterback bootleg. The crowd seemed happy but nervous. Happy to be ahead, but nervous about a slim one-point lead.

After the kickoff the Tigers went three and out and punted to us. The Bulldogs wanted to hang onto the ball and tried desperately to make a first down, but came up short. With three minutes left in the game, I trotted onto the field to punt again.

187

Danny snapped the ball, which landed right in my hands. One step, two steps, BOOT! The ball flew in the air and was fielded by the punt returner at the 20-yard line. Our players ran down the field, but either our team was tired or their return man had gotten a burst of energy. He dodged several tacklers and weaved behind three blockers, who cleared out some running space for him.

Suddenly, the only thing that stood between him and the goal line was me. I was an offensive player, never really trained to tackle, but that didn't matter right now. I needed to make a play or we could kiss the championship goodbye. I thought of the bighorn sheep in Elko's experiments and threw myself headlong at the runner. I careened into him waist-high, knocking him out of bounds and into a cameraman from the local TV station.

Next thing I knew, Bulldogs were surrounding me, jumping up and down with mixed emotions: horror at the long runback and jubilation over my touchdown-saving tackle.

The Tigers, however, had no mixed emotions. They were clearly energized by the long run-back. And to our incredible dismay, a couple of plays later they were at the nine-yard line. First and goal.

"DE-FENSE, DE-FENSE!" shouted the Bulldog crowd.

The Tigers handed it off to their fullback, who was stuffed at the line of scrimmage. Our defense bottled them up on the next two plays as well.

Their kicking unit ran onto the field. I watched as my Tigers counterpart lined up for the kick. I glanced across the field at Elko. He was biting what was left of his nails.

The ball was snapped. One step, two steps, BOOT! I watched as the ball sailed through the goalposts. The Tiger players swarmed around the kicker in glee. The cheers from the Tigers side of the stands was almost deafening.

The Tigers were ahead 38–37, with 1:45 left in the game.

This development was devastating. It knocked the wind out of us for a minute or two. We called a time-out, to get our heads together and formulate a quick plan for getting downfield. We weren't going to give up. We hadn't played this hard for this long, just to quit now. We were going to win this one for the Gipper, or the Gripper, or whomever.

We just wanted the ball back.

The Tigers kicked off, and Tommy ran the ball out to the 25-yard line. We were stuffed at the line of scrimmage on the next two plays. On the following play, Mullen hit Mondo for a short pass, but the defense was ready and tackled him immediately. It was fourth down and seven. For what threatened to be the last play of the game, we called a risky reverse play. Andy Castro ran to the left as if he were running a sweep, but he discreetly handed the ball to Tommy, who had lined up as a flankerback and was running the opposite direction. At first the play looked like it would lose yardage, but Tommy was able to shake the defensive end and find open field.

The crowd went wild as they watched Tommy sprinting downfield, his shoulder pads heaving up and down with each stride. Unfortunately, the Tigers had one man deep in their backfield, who was able to make the tackle. But it was a first down! We had new life. However, our joy was quickly dampened by one thing: the clock. There were eight seconds left in the game.

Coach used another time-out. We called a pass play, trying to hit Mondo on a post route toward the end zone. The ball was broken up by the defender. Now there were four seconds left on the clock.

Once again, Coach called time-out. We huddled up on the sidelines, waiting for the word from Coach, who stared back at us with an almost bemused look. He looked like he was searching for the right words, when I heard Tommy pipe up from my left side.

"Let Ivan kick it," he said. "He's been our go-to guy this season."

"Yeah, Super Booter," chimed in the left tackle Moyers.

"Hold on, boys. I make the decisions around here." Coach

paused, and we all waited. "Ivan," said Coach, "I hope you've had your two bowls of oatmeal today."

"I have," I said. I swallowed hard.

"Great. Now go out there and boot it through the uprights," he said, his voice rising to a shout. "Let's win this one!"

"Yeah! Super Booter," shouted the entire huddle as we ran out onto the field.

I had been nervous thinking I *might* be called upon to make a long-distance field goal. Now that we had *decided* upon a long-distance field goal, my nervousness was replaced by an all-consuming feeling of dread. My stomach felt like I had swallowed a dead cat. The jig was up. I was Super Booter no longer, and soon everyone would know. Unless there was some last-minute reprieve, I was doomed. Nothing left to do but go out there and kick. Maybe if I used all my reserves of gorilla and human strength, I could muster the strength to kick it 47 yards. But I seriously doubted it.

The Tigers might have noticed that I looked ready to kick and decided to ice me by calling time-out. Or maybe they wanted to rearrange their defensive scheme. Perhaps they just wanted to exhaust the Super Booter cheering section. We wandered over to the sideline to wait for the time-out to end, and huddled up around Coach. There wasn't much else he could say. And he didn't want to cloud our minds with too much information. Our mission was simple: block the Tigers' defense and kick a field goal.

"Everyone have their blocking assignment?" asked Coach. "Alright, let's go out there and finish this game with a win!"

We ran out onto the field. I looked downfield at the goalposts. They had never looked farther away. Danny Mapu jogged onto the field next to me. He looked a little nervous. After all, he had no experience in big games.

"Just do what you've been doing all along," I said.

Danny nodded his head and thanked me. Then he turned and jogged toward the line of scrimmage. I walked up to Mullen, who was on one knee preparing for the snap. "You can do it, Super Booter," he said. "You've done it before."

35.

I paced off three long, backward steps and two steps to the left, took a deep breath, and stood on the turf, arms loose by my sides.

As I faced downfield, I could see the Tigers' defensive line, all wired up, ready for the snap. It looked like they were trying to flood the left side of the line. They were going for the block.

"Thirty-five, blue 83," I shouted. "Hut, hut, HUT!"

Our second-string center once again snapped the ball perfectly, except for one important thing. One *very* important thing. Our inexperienced freshman center snapped it to *ME*! He was supposed to snap it to Mullen, the holder. This was not a punt. This was the most important field goal of the season!

Maybe he was so used to snapping it to me that he made a rookie mistake. Maybe he just over-snapped the ball. But there was no time to analyze the mistake. The ball was in my hands, and I had to do something with it. In the old days, the kicker could drop-kick the ball. But I had absolutely no idea how to do that.

I was going to have to run with the ball.

I saw that most of the Tigers were streaming through from my left. My heart leapt into my throat. Suddenly, all the strange sensations in my right leg had vanished. My entire mind and body were consumed with one impulse only. RUN!

My legs blazing, I scrambled around the right side. Luckily, Mondo realized that the ball had not been kicked. He blocked the defensive end toward the middle of the field, slowing him down just enough to let me slip past.

Suddenly, I was running in the open field. I could almost feel the burn of adrenaline in the back of my throat as I tried to pour on the speed. Fortunately, the Tigers' plan was to rush everyone to block the kick, so all of their players were behind me.

Or so I thought! I saw the strong safety sprinting across the field as I approached the 25-yard line. He had the angle on me. There was no way I could beat him to the end zone.
I cut back, hoping that his momentum would carry him past me. And it worked. But it gave time for the other safety, the free safety, to catch me. He dove for my legs and snagged me by the ankle. I hopped up and down with my other foot, dragging the safety with me. On the third hop, I was finally able to struggle free.

But not in time. The strong safety had cut back and was running full speed at me. My heart sank. Despite my outrageous efforts, I would come up five yards short, I realized. The clock had wound down to zero. The Tigers would win.

I took one step and prepared for the hit and... *WHAM!*

I don't know where he came from, but Tommy Dittmore landed a huge block on the strong safety! They both fell to the turf as I ran past.

I saw the end zone and leapt for it, but in the air I felt arms wrap around my body like a straitjacket. I thought it must have been the other defensive players, who had caught up with me. I pulled forward and contorted as I fell, landing face up on the turf, a pile of players on top of me.

Everything was strangely silent and dark. It stayed like that for a moment. I felt oddly at peace under the pile of players, like I was back in the womb.

I could see glimmers of light as the referee pulled players from the top of the pile. One by one, players were yanked to their feet. I could hear the noise of the crowd, but it didn't sound like cheering. I didn't know what it sounded like. It was if I were in another world. As the last player was pulled off me, I looked into brilliant sunlight.

Holding the football tight to my chest like a teddy bear, I

slowly focused my eyes on the black-and-white-striped shirt of the referee who was standing above me. He looked down on me for what seemed like a minute, but was probably only a second. Then he raised both hands in the air.

"Touchdown!" he shouted.

The roar of the crowd sounded like a tidal wave hitting the beach. It was over. We had won the game. And the championship!

It took me a moment, but I finally rose to my feet and looked at the roaring crowd. I jumped up, threw the ball as high as I could, and flung both arms in the air.

Next thing I knew, I was tackled again...by my own team! They practically suffocated me as they mobbed me in the end zone. I finally struggled to my feet. Everyone was ecstatic. No one could even use words. It was all whoops, cheers, and the outrageous laughter of disbelief. But it was true. I had fallen across the goal line and we, the Bulldogs, had won the championship.

I heard Tommy say, "Way to go, Super Booter."

"Unbelievable!" shouted Rensler.

"You rock," shouted Zeph.

I saw Reggie Mapu limping across the field as fast as his injured leg would carry him. Despite his hurt leg, he was so excited that he jumped on me, knocking me down. I found myself on the bottom of a pile, again.

This time it was Coach who pulled them off. Like before, I could see little glimmers of light as each player was pulled off the pile. One of the last players pulled off seemed like an enormous player, much bigger than any of the guys on my team. But I could only focus on him for a second, before Coach grabbed me.

"Super Booter! I knew you'd come through one way or another," he shouted.

Coach, of course, was thrilled. He smacked me on the shoulder pads and hugged me.

"That was incredible! We need to call more broken plays." He laughed.

Finally, I was able to take off my helmet. I gave Coach a double high-five and another hug.

"Thanks for having so much faith in us," I said.

Coach gave me that noble, magnificent Coach smile. But the excitement was too much for even Coach. He let out a loud whoop. "Way to go Bulldogs!" he shouted and hugged me again.

I turned around, and before me stood the gigantic player. His uniform was so small on him that it looked like a kid's Halloween costume. His face was almost crushed up against his facemask.

"Great run, kid!" came a familiar voice.

"Elko," I hissed. "How did you get on the field?"

"The assistant coach let me on. I told him I was your uncle."

"And he let you on the field?"

"No, but I snuck onto the field anyway. He might have seen me jump over the railing, but since I fit in…"

"You fit in like a meatball in a punchbowl," I said. "Where'd you get the uniform?"

"In the locker room. I was going to help kick, remember? I was going to run onto the field, but Dr. Carlson talked me out of it. Well, actually he grabbed the knockout gas and threatened to spray me."

I laughed and thanked the football gods that Dr. Carlson had decided to attend the game.

Players were still leaping around, hugging and high-fiving each other, and the crowd continued to cheer. I heard someone call my name, and I turned around and saw Danny Mapu.

"Sorry about that snap," he said.

"You almost got me killed," I laughed. "I never ran so hard in my life."

"I don't know what I was thinking."

"Don't apologize," I said. "Between me and you, I don't

think I could have made that field goal. Maybe at some psychic level you knew that."

Suddenly Tommy Dittmore, Andy Castro, and Zeph grabbed me by my waist and hoisted me up on Elko's shoulders.

"Super Booter, Super Booter, ooh, aah," I heard as the crowd shouted and stomped their feet. The sound was ecstatic, practically deafening, but completely intoxicating.

The entire team passed by the stands. The crowd cheered for the entire team, for the entire season. We'd won the championship for the first time in our school's history.

Later, the whole team met up at the Haven, where we celebrated until closing time. Kipper, Zeph, Tommy, and I shared a table. We didn't have to pay for a thing all night. Neither did anyone else on the team. My "uncle" showed up around 7:30 and picked up the tab. And he was the last one to leave.

36.

A week after the big game, I got a call from Elko. He wanted me to come down to the stadium, said there was something he wanted to show me.

"I'll come right over," I said. "I need to stop by the lab and get a shot from Dr. Carlson, but I'll stop at the stadium first."

"I'll be waiting for you," said Elko, and he hung up.

When I got there Elko was out on the field, on the 40-yard line, dressed in a T-shirt and sweats. Ipoo was nearby, watching him. Neither of them saw me, so I had a candid view of the action. Elko held a football in his hands. It looked like he was squeezing both ends of the ball, something that kickers do to loosen up the ball. He placed the ball on the tee, jogged back ten yards. Then he turned around and raised his hand.

He leaned forward, intending to run toward the ball, but Ipoo wandered in front of him.

"Move back," he shouted. I could hear him loud and clear across the field.

Then, with big loping strides, Elko ran at the ball and gave it a mighty kick. The ball flew forward like it was shot from a cannon. It didn't go straight, but *wow,* did it go far. I thought it would sail into the seats, but it hit the wall in the corner of the end zone.

Ipoo ran after the ball. I guess he was working as Elko's retriever that day.

"Dang, Elko! You walloped that one," I said as I neared him.

"That's not even close to my best. You remember how I accidentally injected myself with gorilla serum at the game?"

"How could I forget?" I said.

"Well, I thought I'd test out *my* kicking game. Watch this," he said, grinning.

Ipoo came bounding up and put the ball on the tee. Elko walked back ten yards, raised his hand up, took a deep breath, and let out his blood-curdling silverback war cry. Then he ran forward and booted the ball with all his might. The power behind the kick was incredible, if not downright frightening. His accuracy, however, left something to be desired. Again, the ball flew like a cannon shot, this time leaving the field in the corner of the end zone and landing halfway up the stands.

"Ha-ha! How do you like that?" shouted Elko, beaming with pride.

"That's impressive," I said. "But can you warn me next time you do the silverback war cry?"

"Of course not. The element of surprise is essential to the silverback war cry."

"I pity the fan that could have been sitting in that seat," I said, pointing to where the ball was still bouncing around in the stands.

Elko smiled proudly. He was anxious to try another kickoff, but when he looked around, Ipoo was nowhere to be found.

"Ipoo, where are you?" shouted Elko.

We looked around, scanning the stadium in all directions, but there was no sign of the monkey. We were beginning to get worried when Ipoo cautiously poked his head around one of the blocking dummies on the sidelines. He'd been hiding there. Apparently, he wasn't a fan of the silverback war cry either.

"Come here, Ipoo. There's nothing to worry about," said Elko. Ipoo trotted over.

"How did you convince Ipoo to shag the balls for you? Did you threaten him with the knockout spray?" I asked.

"Nah, I stopped doing that. It's probably not good for him. Besides, the spray is expensive to make. I need to conserve it."

"So I guess he trusts you," I said. "That's good to hear."

"Thanks, kid," Elko said. "There's something else you

should know. I've decided to donate 25 percent of my winnings to your football team, so they can fix up that locker room. That place is disgusting. Even for me. It smelled like the monkey house in the zoo. No offense, Ipoo," said Elko, tapping Ipoo on the head.

"Elko, that's very generous. You might have a heart after all."

"Don't tell anyone," he said.

"What? That you have a heart, or that you made a donation to the football team?" I asked.

"Don't tell people I have a heart. It's bad for my image. You can tell everyone I made a donation to the football team. I want the locker room named after me."

I laughed. Elko dug into his pocket, pulled out a roll of money, and handed me two crisp $100 bills.

"This is for all the shoes you had to buy."

I smiled. "Thanks. I appreciate it."

"Let me tell you something, kid," said Elko as he put his big hand on my shoulder. "You're a trouper. I won't forget what you did. It couldn't have been easy living with a gorilla leg for a couple of months."

"Thanks, Elko," I said. I was almost touched.

A football stadium is a strange place when the stands are

empty and there are only a couple of people—and a monkey—milling around the field. We watched a group of seven or eight seagulls circle the field and land near the 30-yard line. They pecked at something in the grass and chased one another around. Finally they flew away, only to land in the end zone, continuing their scavenging.

"What are you going to do with the rest of the money you made, if you don't mind my asking?" I asked Elko.

"I'm going to market the knockout spray, and maybe invest in some drug therapies that Dr. Carlson and I have been developing. This gorilla research might just pay off. And with the rest of the money, I'll just treat myself. I'll live like King Elko for a while. Then it's back to work," he said.

"Sounds like a plan to me," I said.

"Yep," he said, watching the seagulls fly off again.

Meanwhile, Ipoo returned with the ball. Elko gripped it in both hands, gave it a firm squeeze, walked over to the tee, and set it up. He paced backward ten yards.

"Now watch this," said Elko. His eyes were like laser beams focused on the ball. "I think I've been kicking a little high on the ball, so on this one I'll try to kick it a little lower. We'll see how far it will go."

He looked more than determined this time; he looked

downright possessed. Head down, he ran full speed at the ball. With a giant leap, he planted his left foot and whipped his big right leg at the ball. Unfortunately, his kicking foot hit the turf about a foot in front of the ball, sending a divot the size of a winter coat lofting through the air. The massive chuck of sod landed five yards downfield, while the ball tumbled along the ground ahead of it.

"Bah!" Elko shouted.

"It takes practice," I said.

"That's why I asked you to come down here. I want you to teach me a few of the fundamentals," said Elko. "Then I might join the team next year."

I looked at him skeptically.

"I'm kidding," he said.

"Good," I said. "You had me worried for a second. How about I stop by the laboratory and get a shot from Dr. Carlson first. Then we'll have a little practice."

"Good idea," said Elko. "But before you go, could you hold the ball so I could try to kick a field goal?"

"You've got to be kidding," I said, astonished. "You'll probably miss the ball and kick me with your size-15 foot. Then, *I'll* go sailing through the goalposts. You've got to work on your control first."

"Oh, c'mon," he said. "I won't kick you."

"No way."

"Alright," said Elko, waving me off. "Go see Dr. Carlson and then come back here. I'll be waiting."

"Give me an hour."

"You got it, kid," said Elko. "Maybe you should run. I never knew you were such a good runner until that game on Saturday." He laughed. Then he turned around and punted the ball, a boomer that landed in the stands.

37.

I flashed my zoo membership card at the entrance and wandered into the zoo. The day was unseasonably warm and sunny, and a good-size crowd was meandering down the walkways. People were eating popcorn and ice cream cones and congregating at the various exhibits. I looked across a big patio at the grassy area where we had pitched our tents during the Zoo Night campout. I let out a sigh. It had been a long two months since that unforgettable night.

I was early for my appointment with Dr. Carlson, so I walked past the bear enclosures and the petting zoo. For old time's sake, I strolled over to the gorilla enclosure. Who did I see? Dr. Carlson, observing the gorillas.

He saw me and waved, then walked over. "How are you feeling?" he asked.

"Like an enormous weight has been lifted from my shoulders," I said. "Don't get me wrong. It was a lot of fun being Super Booter. I'm glad I had the experience. But I wouldn't want to do it again. Having a gorilla leg is very stressful. Lots of unknown factors involved."

"You realize that it's still top secret information, don't you?"

"Yes. And that's the other thing. Except for you and Elko, I can't even talk about it with anyone. Do you know what it's like carrying a secret like that?"

"It must eat at you."

"Like a nest of termites."

"So what are you going to do about next football season? Will the fans expect a return of Super Booter?"

I hadn't given it much thought. Certainly the team would expect the return of Super Booter, and when he didn't arrive, they would be disappointed and questions would arise.

"We can give you gorilla genes again," smirked Dr. Carlson.

"No thanks," I said. "I'll deal with it somehow."

We looked into the enclosure. Three gorillas—a juvenile, a female, and the big silverback—stood in the shade of a leafy tree. The female and the juvenile sat on a barren patch of ground, while the silverback stood on all fours. They didn't utter a sound or move a muscle. They stood motionless, staring back at us. Dr. Carlson and I observed them for a long while.

"I wonder what they are thinking," said Dr. Carlson, finally.

"I don't know, but I think I came a little too close to finding out."

Dr. Carlson laughed. We walked back to the lab, discussing the ramifications of my gorilla leg and whether we could use my experiences as scientific data. Given the top secret nature of the mission, he wondered when, if ever, he could make the information public.

Later, after I had received my injection, I walked down to the stadium to meet Elko again. This time I stopped in the locker room. One thing I could say for this old, dingy place—the lockers were big. I had left all kinds of clothing and other items in my locker.

I opened it and took out my helmet, jersey, and shoulder pads. I found my football pants and changed into them. I pulled out my old, size 10 game shoes and dropped them onto the floor, pieces of dried dirt and grass scattering across the concrete. Sitting on the bench, I stared at my shoes for a moment, thinking about the whole ordeal—the visits to the lab, the games, the shaved legs and the new shoes.

From the field outside, a silverback war cry snapped me out of my daydream. Elko was waiting.

I laughed to myself and began putting on my shoes. I rose to my feet and jumped up and down a few times. I patted both shoes for good luck. And you know what? They felt great as I walked out of the locker room and onto the playing field.

Thanks

I'd like to thank Brent Baumann, a high school referee and a great source of information about high school football. Also, big thanks to Ricki Colman of the Wisconsin National Primate Research Center who knows an awful lot about macaques and was happy to share that information with me. If there have been excessive liberties taken with the rules of the high school game or the mannerisms of macaques, the blame lies with the author - not with Brent or Ricki.